Forever

A

STALLION

Deborah Fletcher Mello

HARLEQUIN®
entertain, enrich, inspire™

To Wes "Third" Woody,
You are a source of sheer inspiration.
Your bright smile absolutely moves my spirit.
Please know that you are much loved.

Recycling programs
for this product may
not exist in your area.

ISBN-13: 978-0-373-86270-2

FOREVER A STALLION

Copyright © 2012 by Deborah Fletcher Mello

For questions and comments about the quality of this book, please contact us
at Customer_eCare@Harlequin.ca.

www.Harlequin.com

Printed in U.S.A.

She nodded her head as she eased around him, treading gently to keep from falling into the water.

As she stepped into his space, Mason inhaled the scent of her perfume, a light floral fragrance wafting beneath his nose. Before he realized what he was doing, he clutched her arm, pulling her to him. He hesitated for only a moment, Phaedra meeting his intense stare with a look of her own. Her breath caught deep in her chest, and her heart raced unexpectedly.

Without a second thought, Mason leaned in to kiss her, allowing his lips to lightly graze hers. His breath was hot with wanting, his full lips quivering in anticipation. He pulled away and stared into her eyes a second time and then he dropped his mouth to hers, meeting Phaedra's lips in a deep, soul-searing kiss.

Time seemed to come to a standstill. Phaedra felt as if the world had rotated her into the stratosphere, with everything spinning around her. Mason held her tightly, his hands burning hot against the bare skin of her arms and shoulders. His body melded tight to hers and both were in awe of the sensations, feeling as if they were melting one into the other. When he finally pulled back, both of them gasping for air, he knew beyond any doubt that he had absolutely fallen in love with Phaedra, and Phaedra was falling in love with him.

Books by Deborah Fletcher Mello

Kimani Romance

In the Light of Love
Always Means Forever
To Love a Stallion
Tame a Wild Stallion
Lost in a Stallion's Arms
Promises to a Stallion
Seduced by a Stallion
Forever a Stallion

DEBORAH FLETCHER MELLO

Writing since she was thirteen years old, Deborah Fletcher Mello can't imagine herself doing anything else. Her first romance novel, *Take Me to Heart,* earned her a 2004 Romance Slam Jam nomination for Best New Author. In 2005 she received Book of the Year and Favorite Heroine nominations for her novel *The Right Side of Love,* and in 2009 won an *RT Book Reviews* Reviewer's Choice Award for her ninth novel, *Tame a Wild Stallion.* Most recently Deborah's eleventh novel, *Promises to a Stallion,* has earned her a 2011 Romance Slam Jam nomination for Hero of the Year.

For Deborah, writing is as necessary as breathing and she firmly believes that if she could not write she would cease to exist. Weaving a story that leaves her audience feeling full and complete, as if they've just enjoyed an incredible meal, is an ultimate thrill for her. Born and raised in Connecticut, Deborah now maintains base camp in North Carolina but considers home to be wherever the moment moves her.

Dear Reader,

I have absolutely loved my four billionaire brothers, Matthew, Mark, Luke and John Stallion. With their individual stories finished, I was ready to move on. But something kept pulling at my creative spirit, demanding that I continue what I'd started, and it soon became clear that the Stallion family's story was far from over.

Discovering the illustrious Phaedra Parrish, the one and only Stallion sister, came as a complete and total surprise to me. But as the details of her story unraveled, I found myself completely enthralled. I loved introducing Phaedra to her brothers and watching the new family dynamics unfold.

Forever a Stallion also introduces the Boudreaux family out of New Orleans, opening the door to much, much more to come.

As always, I appreciate the love and support that you continue to show me. I love to hear what you think, so please don't hesitate to contact me at DeborahMello@aol.com.

Until the next time, take care and God bless.

With much love,

Deborah Fletcher Mello

www.deborahmello.blogspot.com

Chapter 1

Mason Boudreaux extended a large hand toward the president and chief executive officer of Stallion Enterprises. John Stallion shook it heartily, cementing his company's five-billion-dollar acquisition of the Boudreaux hotel chain.

"Congratulations!" Mason intoned as John's brother, Matthew Stallion, popped the cork on a vintage bottle of Veuve Clicquot Brut champagne.

John nodded. "And congratulations to you, as well, sir. I'm sure this means that you will be wearing retirement quite well."

"I don't know about retirement." Mason let out a deep chuckle. "But I imagine I'm going to have a hell of a time with whatever my next business venture might be."

Matthew passed each man a crystal flute filled with drink. "Well, Mason, if your next adventure is as profitable as this one was, you'll be doing exceptionally well for yourself, my friend."

Mason nodded his agreement as he lifted his champagne glass in salute, celebrating the sale of his hotel-owning company to the Stallion family. At his age of thirty-seven, selling the forty-five hundred hotels that constituted Boudreaux International Hotels and Resorts was a testament to his hard work and dedication. The multibillion-dollar payment was an acknowledgment of his success.

"And now that Boudreaux International is under the Stallion umbrella, I can only hope and pray that we will continue to build on all of your accomplishments," John said, grinning broadly, "which is why I'm happy that we could convince you to stay on board in a consulting capacity. I'm certain that we'll need to draw on your knowledge and experience."

Mason took a sip of his drink. "It's going to be a great partnership and I'm glad we're keeping it in the family," he said as he gestured in Matthew's direction.

Matthew laughed. "I appreciate that, brother-in-law. More than you know."

"Oh, I know!" Mason said, laughing with him. "I know my sister. I'm sure Katrina has just about worked your last nerve offering her advice about this deal. I've lost count of the number of times she's wrangled me to give her opinion."

"You know it!" Matthew said, thinking of his beautiful new wife. Mason's sister Katrina and he had married a few weeks earlier. His whirlwind relationship with the district court judge had taken them both by surprise and now the couple was anxiously awaiting

the arrival of their first child together. "And those preg-
nancy hormones have not helped."

The third oldest Stallion brother, Mark, chimed
in as he stepped through the conference room door.
His baby daughter was clutched to his chest, the six-
month-old little girl looking around in wide-eyed wonder. "Well, the wives are headed upstairs. Good news
traveled fast."

"I swear, it's like they all have radar." John laughed
and shook his head. He leaned to nuzzle his niece's
chubby cheek.

"I heard that, John Stallion," his wife, Marah, said
as she led the way into the oversize room.

John laughed as the beautiful woman moved to his
side. He leaned to kiss her lips, wrapping his arms
tightly around her small frame. "I didn't say anything,
baby!"

Marah rolled her eyes as she kissed him back. "Uh-
huh. Sure you didn't!"

Mark's wife, Michelle Stallion, waved her hand in
greeting as she brought up the rear. "Hey, everyone,"
she said brightly as she reached to take her daughter
from her husband's arms. Mark wrapped them both in
a deep bear hug.

"Congratulations!" Katrina shouted. She moved to
kiss her brother's cheek first and then her husband's.
"This is so exciting!" she said as she nestled close
against Matthew's chest.

Matthew caressed the bulge of new baby that pro-
truded from her abdomen, his fingers lingering where
the baby kicked once, and then a second time. "Yes,
it is!"

With the arrival of the women, the chatter in the

room rose exponentially. Mason was feeling right at home as he looked around at the gleaming faces. Family—the best cheerleaders any man could wish for. He and his sister Katrina came from a large family, so this felt very much like home to them both. He grinned widely as he noted the endearing gestures she and her husband exchanged.

He couldn't help being in awe of the wealth of love that filled the room. With Matthew and Katrina; John and his wife, Marah; and Mark, his wife, Michelle, and their new baby girl, Irene, the room overflowed with love.

Mason was suddenly introspective as he imagined what it might be like to have someone of his own to love. He had mastered professional success to the detriment of his personal life. Although he'd enjoyed the many beautiful women who had gone hand in hand with his lifestyle, he'd grown weary of the endless workweeks and his playboy lifestyle. Mason found himself not only ready for a change, but actively searching for the comforts family and stability would afford him. Selling his business could not have come at a more opportune time. He could feel himself grinning at the prospects.

His thoughts were interrupted by the persistent chatter. He shifted forward in his seat as he drew his focus back to the conversation.

"Where's Luke?" Katrina was asking. "And Joanne? I thought they'd be here."

John shook his head. "Last-minute wedding chores. They had to have their final session of couple's counseling with Reverend Barnes, and this was the only time he could fit them in. They'll catch up with us all later."

"Speaking of chores," Marah interjected. "We ladies have a very long list of things to get done. Between the rodeo and the wedding, we'll be running from one event to the next through the end of the month, and that takes some preparing for. Each one of us is going to need a few new outfits to wear. Isn't that right?" she said as Michelle and Katrina nodded in agreement.

Mark winked toward his brothers, shaking his head. "I told Luke to elope but no, you women had to throw in your two cents. He and Joanne could have been married by now. Done and finished. Then none of you would need to do any shopping at all!"

John laughed. "Do not get these women started, please."

Marah tapped John against the chest. "You've got some nerve."

"Don't pay either one of them any attention," Katrina said, rolling her eyes skyward. "Matthew will tell you that he enjoyed every second of our wedding. Didn't you, honey?"

Matthew leaned to kiss her cheek. "That's right, my darling! Walking down the aisle with you was the best thing I ever did," he said, winking at the men.

Mason chuckled. "It sounds to me like you guys have your hands full."

Matthew's head bobbed up and down. "Oh, no, not at all," he said, his eyes widening mischievously as Katrina punched him playfully in the arm.

Mason grinned broadly as he watched his sister and brother-in-law, the two teasing each other playfully. It had been a long time since he'd seen Katrina so happy.

Joy shimmered out of her dark eyes, everything between her and her husband exemplifying the dynamic relationship they shared. An unexpected hint of jealousy flooded Mason's spirit. As if reading his mind, Katrina moved to her big brother's side, wrapping her arm around his broad shoulders.

"There will be a lot of beautiful, successful women for you to meet while you're here in Dallas, Mason," she said casually.

Mason smiled. "Really?" he questioned, crossing his arms over his chest.

Katrina nodded. "You might even find us a new sister-in-law if you play your cards right, big brother!"

Tossing his head back, Mason laughed heartily. Saying nothing aloud, he leaned to kiss his sister's cheek. *From your mouth to God's ears,* he thought to himself, his smile brightening even more. *From your mouth to God's ears!*

Chapter 2

Phaedra Parrish closed and locked the front door of her family home after bidding a member from her mother's church goodbye. People had been popping in to check on her since the funeral, and with the day being her twenty-eighth birthday, there had been a revolving door of family and friends coming to give her support. It had been a long day and an even longer month, and she was glad for the wealth of silence that quickly enveloped the room. She sighed deeply as she dropped down onto the cushioned sofa that sat opposite her mother's favorite rocking chair.

As she stared at the empty seat, Phaedra's tears clouded her dark eyes. It didn't feel as if a whole month had passed since her mother, Arneta Parrish, had last rocked in that chair, everything seemingly well. Then without warning, a pulmonary embolism had taken her away. Their family doctor had reasoned that she'd probably been experiencing symptoms days earlier, the blood clot traveling from her leg to her lung. But Phaedra had not been there to know, and now her mother was gone from her.

Swiping at the tears that fell down her cheeks, Phaedra closed her eyes and inhaled, filling her lungs with a deep breath. She couldn't help wishing that she'd come home as originally scheduled instead of extending her photography assignment those additional days. Had she been home, then just maybe her beloved mother would still be there with her.

Even as the thought crossed her mind, Phaedra could hear her mother admonishing her, the woman's deep alto voice echoing in her thoughts. *"You're wasting time, little girl! Focus on what you need to do and get your narrow behind to doin' somethin' worthwhile."* And just as the thought crossed her mind, she felt a warm breeze blow through the room and a gust of wind gently caressing her cheeks.

Phaedra rose to her feet, wrapping her arms tightly around her torso. Across the room she imagined that her mother's chair was rocking, the movement ever so slight, and she couldn't help smiling, sensing that Miss Arneta was still there, still watching over her, still intent on keeping her on the straight and narrow. She shook her head from side to side as she laughed. "Yes, ma'am," she said out loud, chuckling softly.

Moving through the modest home, Phaedra checked that the lower level was secure, ensuring that all the doors and windows were locked. Leaving the one light on in the hallway, she headed up the stairs, hesitating for a brief moment in front of her mother's bedroom door. She'd known that at some point she would have to sort through her mother's things, and although it wasn't a task Phaedra had looked forward to, she knew it had to be done.

Pushing the door open, Phaedra flicked the light switch on the wall as she moved inside the small room. Dropping down against the full-size mattress, she drew her hands across the handmade quilt that decorated the bed. She missed her mother with a vengeance. Her grief was so consuming that she couldn't imagine how she was going to survive. She let out a deep sigh.

As she moved to stand back up, Phaedra's heel brushed against a large shoe box protruding from beneath the bed. Reaching down, she drew her hand against the exterior surface, pausing as she thought about its contents. She'd found the container while searching for her mother's favorite black heels to take to the undertaker. As she'd scanned the documents inside, none of it had made any sense to her. Refusing to acknowledge what she'd discovered, she'd tossed it to the floor, kicking it back beneath the bed. She'd known that she would eventually have to revisit it all and she'd chosen to ignore it until there was nothing else on her plate to deal with.

Slipping her tank top over her head and stepping out of her shorts, she dropped the garments to the floor. Pulling back the covers, she crawled into her mother's bed, drawing the comforter around her small frame. The box rested against the bed beside her, and her hand shook ever so slightly as she tossed the container's cover to the floor. Pulling the documents into her lap, Phaedra took a deep breath and then a second.

If anyone had asked her about her mother having secrets, Phaedra would have sworn on her own life that there wasn't anything about Arneta Parrish that she didn't know. But Arneta had carried the biggest secret of her life to her grave, never disclosing the bombshell that would soon be her only daughter's life.

Arneta's collection of diaries rested on top. Pulling the leather-bound journals into her hands, Phaedra pulled at a black-and-white photo that served as a page holder for the most recent entry. The image was of her mother and a man Phaedra didn't know, the couple caught in a deep embrace. Her mother was smiling, joy shining in her expression. The handsome man's smile was not as bright, something in his eyes telling a very different story. But he had a kind face and it was obvious that his presence was making her mother very happy.

Flipping the photo over, Phaedra read the name on the back side. James David Stallion. The photo was dated a year before Phaedra was born. Resting the photo back inside the book, she continued to flip through other papers on James Stallion's life.

There was a letter dated just a few short months after the photo, Mr. Stallion apologizing for a quick departure, wishing his dear friend Arneta a bright and successful future. The ink had faded in spots, drops of moisture having dampened the paper. It was obvious her mother had cried over that letter, remnants of her tearstains having marred some of the words.

Tucked in the envelope with that single letter was a yellowed newspaper article that had been folded closed. It was the obituary that carried the news of James Stallion's death. The man had died in a fiery car accident with his beloved wife, Irene, the couple leaving behind four young sons.

Four sons. Four boys who'd grown to be four very successful men. Phaedra's mother had kept tabs on the Stallion kin, collecting articles of their many accomplishments. Flipping through the articles, Phaedra couldn't help being impressed. But she didn't understand her mother's reasons for caring, the woman having never mentioned the family to her daughter. Phaedra had to wonder why.

Adjusting the pillows beneath her head, Phaedra flipped through the diaries until she found the one dated the year before her birth. She opened the journal to the first page, pulling her knees upright as she rested the book against her thighs. She was suddenly anxious to know her mother's secret and the story that she'd never been told. And she was anxious to read them in her mother's own words.

One week later flight number 1267 from New Orleans, Louisiana, to Dallas, Texas, departed, leaving Phaedra with one hour and thirty-five minutes to rethink what she was planning to do before touching down. Her stomach knotted, feeling as if her sugared beignet and chicory coffee breakfast was not going to sit well. Phaedra knew it was only nerves, anxiety pretending to be her new best friend since she'd read her mother's journals, opening a chapter into her own life that she'd not been prepared for.

Phaedra drew her manicured fingers against her Coach bag, two of her mother's journals and some supporting documents secured in a side pocket. It hadn't taken any time at all for her to go through her mother's papers and discover that there had been much about the woman that she hadn't known. The writings had read like a bestselling romance novel, detailing the highs of her mother's relationship with James David Stallion. And then the lows, James David Stallion disappearing from Arneta's life like a dream lost too soon to a morning sunrise. James leaving before ever learning about the child Arneta would eventually raise alone.

James David Stallion. Phaedra's biological father. The secret her mother had never wanted her to know. Phaedra shook her head for the umpteenth time since finding out, her eyes lifting to stare out the airplane window. An endless bright blue sky marred by an occasional tuft of cloud brought a slight smile to her face. The view was magical, soothing the inner turmoil that threatened Phaedra's peace of mind.

All of her life Phaedra had believed that Daniel Parrish had been her father. Daniel Parrish had only been married to her mother for short two years before disappearing into the Louisiana penal system. Reading her mother's story, Phaedra discovered Arneta had already been pregnant when she'd met and married Daniel.

After many years of therapy Phaedra had come to terms with having an absentee father who preferred a life of crime over his loving wife and daughter. Her mother had often used her own life as an example of what happened when a woman made bad choices over men who were not deserving of her. She'd been apologetic for not having served Phaedra better.

When Daniel had died, still locked behind prison walls, Phaedra had mourned the loving father she had wanted him to be, not the apathetic parent he had actually been. And through it all, her mother had never once considered that Phaedra needed to know the truth of her paternity. But reading her mother's words, Phaedra had come to understand that her mother had wanted only to protect both her daughter and James Stallion, the only man she'd apparently ever loved. Holding the truth close to her heart had been Arneta's way of shielding all of them from heartbreak. But Arneta had been wrong because her heart had been broken, and now Phaedra's heart was broken, too.

Heading to Dallas, Phaedra was now hoping for an opportunity to meet the siblings who shared her bloodline. Hoping against all odds to connect with her father's family, the family that was also her own.

Chapter 3

"Wow!" Mason called out, his eyes widening as they settled down against the bleachers to watch the annual Wild West rodeo show that was about to begin. The entire morning had been a whirlwind of events, one happening right after the other. Mason would never have imagined the magnitude of the Briscoe-Stallion Annual Rodeo, it being the most attended community event in Dallas each year.

Briscoe Ranch was well over eight hundred acres of working cattle ranch, an equestrian center and an entertainment complex that specialized in corporate and private client services. With the property being central to Austin, Houston, Dallas and Fort Worth, Briscoe Ranch had made quite a name for itself.

Back in the day, Edward Briscoe, the ranch's original owner, had been one of the original black cowboys. Not long after the birth of his three daughters, Eden and the twins, Marla and Marah, he and his first wife had expanded their Texas longhorn operation, adding two twenty-thousand-square-feet event barns and a country bed-and-breakfast.

After Marah Briscoe's marriage to business tycoon John Stallion, Edward had given the property to his daughter and new son-in-law, her love for a Stallion ending the conflict that had brought the couple together in the first place. Under the Stallion family umbrella, Briscoe Ranch was growing steadily and now a point of consideration for a number of government programs to assist children and families in need. The ranch was home to them all, and the pride and joy of both families.

"This is something!" Mason said, tipping his head toward John and Matthew, who'd settled down beside him.

John laughed. "Marah's father, Edward, has been hosting this event since forever. Every year we're amazed at just how big it's gotten."

Matthew nodded his concurrence. "At the rate we're growing, I'm afraid we might run out of land to accommodate everyone," he said jokingly.

John and Mason both laughed with him.

"So, what then?" Mason queried. "Will you buy the state of Texas?"

John grinned broadly. "Maybe Mexico, too, especially if we keep allowing these women to be in charge!" he mused.

Laughter rang out among them, the three men clearly having a good time.

From a safe distance across the way, Phaedra adjusted the lens on her camera, focusing her sight on the two brothers seated beside each other. She snapped a photo and then a second one before letting the camera rest back against her chest, hanging from a secure leather strap around her neck.

The rodeo event had been a stroke of luck for her. Access to the ranch and the Stallion men had come with minimal difficulty. From the moment Phaedra had stepped onto the property, the brothers had been front and center, taking their hosting responsibilities seriously. Without needing to ask, Phaedra had been able to identify the four of them almost instantly.

From the back pocket of her denim jeans, Phaedra pulled out the photograph she'd found in her mother's possessions, glancing from them to it and back again. There was no mistaking the Stallion lineage detailed in their facial features, each son the spitting image of his father, and hers. Their resemblance to her was even more startling. From the warm coloration of their black-coffee complexions, chiseled jawlines, plush pillows for lips and warm, endearing smiles, Phaedra saw hints of her own reflection. She had their eyes, the same nose, high cheekbones and mouth. Had she inherited her father's dark complexion instead of her mother's milk-chocolate tone, she would easily have passed for a Stallion twin. Phaedra took a deep breath as she suddenly fought not to cry.

Lifting her camera back to her eyes, she peered through the lens, once again pointing it toward where the brothers sat. She focused her gaze on one and then the other. She watched as the brother on the end leaned over to exchange conversation with a man who sat on his sibling's other side. Phaedra shifted her camera and refocused it, zooming in on the stranger. There was something about the handsome man that suddenly had her curious. She couldn't help wondering who he was, his brilliant smile warm and magnanimous.

Whoever the man was, he was quite good-looking, Phaedra thought as she spun the lens into focus, snapping a quick shot and then a second. The trio seemed quite friendly with one another, clearly enjoying the events playing out in the center of the arena. And then, as if his radar had sounded an alarm, the man suddenly looked up, his gaze shifting directly toward her as if he knew she was staring at him. Phaedra lowered her camera abruptly, feeling as if she'd gotten caught with both hands in the cookie jar, her palms overflowing with her favorite oatmeal-raisin treats. She pulled her hands through the length of her hair. The moment was slightly unnerving.

From the ground below, Phaedra suddenly heard her name being called, the sound of it startling her from her thoughts.

"Phaedra? Is that you? Phaedra Parrish!"

Glancing below, she caught sight of the red-haired white man waving wildly for her attention. His own cameras hung down against his side as he struggled not to drop them. Phaedra's eyes widened brightly, the familiar face warming her spirit.

"Hooper!" Phaedra squealed, waving back. She eased her way down from the bleachers to move to the man's side.

With his mane of fire-engine-red hair and the pipe that hung from his mouth like an appendage, Hooper Mars was a welcome sight, looking more like a lumberjack right out of the thick of a deep forest than the award-winning photographer that he was. Hooper's brilliant smile put Phaedra instantly at ease. As she stepped off the last plank, the man wrapped her in a deep bear hug.

Her mentor in art school, Hooper was single-handedly responsible for Phaedra changing her major from creative writing to photography. The two had become fast friends, he challenging her creative spirit and she excelling beyond his expectations. Phaedra's successful career had only been rivaled by his.

"Watch the camera!" Phaedra laughed, lifting the device above her head as she hugged him tightly.

"Nice equipment," Hooper responded, eyeing her Canon 5D Mark II full-frame camera with its long telephoto lens.

Phaedra adjusted her Lowepro camera backpack against her shoulder. "Thanks. What are you doing here?" she asked, surprise still ringing in her tone.

"Working. You?"

"Not working!" Phaedra said with a smile.

"So, what brings you all the way to Dallas and to here of all places?"

Phaedra hesitated, her shoulders shrugging skyward. "I was just passing through town before I head to my next gig in Thailand and I heard about the rodeo. Thought I'd stop by to check it out. See what I might be able to shoot," she said, hoping she sounded believable.

Her friend nodded his understanding. "I was really sorry to hear about your mother, Phaedra. She was a really sweet lady."

Phaedra took a deep breath and forced her mouth into a slight smile. "Thanks, Hooper. And thank you for the flowers! I really appreciated you thinking of me."

"Hey, what are friends for?" the man said. There

was a sudden rush of noise behind them as the audience cheered something going on in the center of the arena. Both Phaedra and Hooper both turned to stare as a horse and rider went through their paces.

"I should be shooting this," Phaedra said absently, her gaze shifting for a split second toward the stands and the men who were still sitting in observation.

"Speaking of shoot, I loved that LeBron James layout you did for *Sports Illustrated*. Creative, challenging, technically proficient. That was some nice work, woman. That shot where you had him hanging upside down from the basketball hoop was seriously dope!"

Phaedra turned her attention back to her friend. "Thank you! It was fun to do and LeBron was a dream client. So, what are you working on here?"

"I'm here to shoot the wedding."

Phaedra eyed him curiously. "What wedding?"

"The Stallion wedding. I'm the wedding photographer."

Phaedra laughed. "I didn't know you did weddings."

Hooper shrugged. "I usually don't, not in a good long time, but I bend the rules for my very special friends. The bride," he said, lifting his eyebrows, "is Joanne Lake. We were roomies for a short time back in Cali when she was going to art school and I was aspiring to make movies."

"I didn't know you made movies."

Hooper laughed. "It was a very short porn career because I was very short."

Phaedra shook her head, laughing with him. "So, this Joanne Lake is getting married to one of the Stallions?"

"Yep!" Hooper nodded. "The youngest brother, Luke Stallion. Great guy! They make a nice couple."

Phaedra felt her heart skip a quick beat. Knowing where she fell in the lineup of Stallion offspring had been a point of angst for her mother. During their short tryst, James Stallion had been married, the truth of that coming as a complete surprise. Although he'd been separated from his wife during the time they were together, the revelation of his marital connection had not sat well with the matriarch. James returning to his wife and three older sons had been earth-shattering, completely devastating Arneta's world. Now here Phaedra was, discovering that her younger brother was about to be married. She took a deep breath, holding it for a brief moment before blowing the air out slowly.

"Hey," Hooper said suddenly. "What are you doing tonight? You interested in working?"

Phaedra lifted her eyebrows questioningly. "What do you need?"

"I have an assistant who will be helping me, but I could always use another photographer. You interested in working? I mean, since you already have your equipment with you."

"At the wedding?"

"The wedding and the reception. You game?"

Taking another quick glance toward where the Stallion men were seated, Phaedra suddenly saw opportunity where none had existed before. Unable to resist, she took note of the handsome stranger one last time, then without a second thought nodded, her answer emphatic. "Yes!"

Joanne Lake stood in the center of the room, a hand fanning in front of her face as she tried to catch her breath.

"I swear," she said, breathing heavily, "I'm so nervous that I can't breathe!"

Marah laughed, moving to the young woman's side. "I felt the same way when John and I were married," she said, remembering the moment as if it had just happened. "Just take a deep breath, hold it and relax. Everything is going to be perfect."

"Absolutely," Joanne's mother, Lillian Taylor, echoed as she slowly laced the back of her only daughter's wedding gown. "Everything will be beautiful, *ma fille chéri,*" the woman said, the warm lilt of her deep French accent comforting.

Tears misted in Joanne's eyes as she took in her image in the mirror. The gown she'd designed for herself accentuated every ounce of her curvaceous frame. She was an absolutely stunning bride in the silk-and-organza creation and she couldn't wait for Luke to see her coming down the aisle that very first time. She took in a deep breath, fighting to ease the rise of nervous energy.

There was a low knock at the door and Marah's older sister, Eden, moved to see who was waiting on the other side. When Eden pulled the entrance open, Phaedra was smiling brightly, waving her camera in greeting.

"Hi, I've come to take some preliminary shots of the bride, if that's okay?" Phaedra said, meeting Eden's questioning gaze.

"Oh, yes, definitely," the woman responded as she reached for Phaedra's hand and pulled her into the room. "Your timing is perfect."

Phaedra nodded as she entered the space, the women inside all turning to stare in her direction. Joanne's bright smile eased the moment.

"Hi, I'm Joanne. Hooper said you'd be coming. It's such a pleasure to meet you," she said excitedly.

"It's nice to meet you, too. My name's Phaedra. Phaedra Parrish," she said, pausing momentarily as if she hoped there might be some recognition that she was family, too. "Congratulations!"

"Thank you," Joanne intoned. "Thank you so much. Well, just tell us where you want us."

Phaedra smiled back. "I just want you to finish getting dressed. Just interact the way you were doing before I arrived and pretend I'm not even here. The best shots are those where you're most natural, so just be yourself."

Joanne nodded as her mother moved back to lacing the last few ties on her gown. As she did, Phaedra lifted her camera and took a quick shot. She began to slowly move around the room, snapping photo after photo of Joanne and her bridal party as they completed the finishing touches on their makeup and hair. It was an extravaganza of ivory-colored lace, chocolate charmeuse and tan chiffon.

"This is so exciting!" Katrina commented, smoothing the front of her own gown across her pregnant belly.

"This family has definitely had its fair share of weddings and baby showers!" an elderly woman intoned. "It's been a blessing!" She swiped at a tear that pressed anxiously at the edge of her eye.

Phaedra paused to look where the voice had come from. Seated on the couch was a woman close to her mother's age. She looked quite smart in a two-piece dress suit the color of sweet tea. She smiled when she saw Phaedra staring. Phaedra smiled back as she lifted her camera and took a snapshot of the woman's smiling face.

"Don't you start crying, Aunt Juanita," someone scolded. "If you start you'll have us all crying up in here."

The women all laughed, the warmth of it echoing around the room.

"Y'all know I'm gonna cry," the woman named Juanita said. "The last of my babies is getting married," she said with a loud sniffle. A blanket of silence dropped down against the room as they all stopped to take in her comment.

Phaedra's gaze danced from face to face as she took them all in. Juanita caught her staring and Phaedra fiddled with her camera as the woman stared back.

"Are you from around here?" Juanita asked, her question directed at Phaedra.

The young woman met the matriarch's curious gaze. "No, ma'am. I'm from New Orleans," she said softly.

Juanita smiled, still staring. "You look like you could be related to the family," she said, "like one of the cousins. Doesn't she?" Juanita queried, moving the rest of them to turn and stare a second time.

Joanne glanced in Phaedra's direction. "You really do," she said with a slight giggle.

Phaedra only smiled, resuming her picture-taking.

Marah interrupted the moment. "It's time, ladies. This wedding will start on time," she said, her tone commanding as she shifted into wedding planner mode.

There were nods of agreement as each woman paused to take one last look at her reflection in the wall of mirrors that decorated the space.

The woman they called Aunt Juanita stood up, moving to the center of the room toward the bride, who suddenly looked as if she'd turned two shades of green.

"Everyone join hands," Juanita said as she gestured for them to move into a circle around Joanne.

Phaedra moved back against the wall, mindful not to intrude upon the moment. She listened intently as the woman began to speak, her camera at eye level as she captured the moment on film.

"This family is a beautiful thing to behold," Juanita said. "I have watched John, Matthew, Mark and Luke grow into wonderful men. I know that if their parents were here today they would be very proud. Each of them has chosen an amazing, wonderful woman to carry the Stallion name and be with them by their sides. They got that from their daddy because their mother, Irene, was an amazing woman and the best friend I could ever have had."

Juanita paused to press a lace hankie to her eye. Her gaze paused on each face as she called out their names. "Marah, Michelle, Katrina and now Joanne, each of you is the most important thing in your husband's life and the lifelines that will continue this family. Don't you ever forget it and don't ever let anyone tell you otherwise.

"Marah, business is important to John, but it will never be more important than you are. Mitch," she said, calling Michelle by her family nickname, "I never thought there would be anyone who could tame that wild Stallion, but you did, and Mark's love for you and that baby girl of yours has no limits.

"Katrina, you told me on your wedding day that Matthew seduced you, but you're the one who actually swept Matthew off his feet. I have never seen him happier." Juanita reached for Joanne's hand, squeezing the woman's fingers beneath her own. "And now our baby boy is getting married. Joanne, you and Luke were both lost until you found each other's arms for support. He is a better man because of you and I couldn't be more proud.

"So, baby girl, you enjoy every minute of this very special day. May you and Luke grow in your love for each other and may you both find joy and happiness for the rest of your days. Welcome to our family. We love you and we couldn't be happier for you both."

"Amen to that," Marah chimed, everyone echoing those sentiments.

Joanne fanned her hands in front of her face, fighting not to bawl like a newborn baby. "Thank you," she said, fighting back the tears. "I love you all so much," she said as her mother wrapped her in a warm embrace.

Juanita moved toward the door. "Well, let's go get you married!" she said, the rest of them following behind her.

And as they moved out of the room, in the direction of the family chapel, Phaedra swiped the tears from her own eyes, snapping one more photo for the Stallion wedding album.

Chapter 4

Mason Boudreaux was all partied out as he moved from the tented reception area back toward the Stallion family home. Guests were still enjoying the Stallion hospitality as they moved from the banquet tables laden with a surplus of food to the dance floor and back again.

Outside, the sun was in the final moments of its descent, the backdrop of a darkening sky heightening the rise of an almost full moon. Small white lights twinkled from the trees that lined the property, casting a seductive glow over the landscape. Looking out over the magnificent view, he couldn't help being touched by the magnitude of it all. He took a deep breath, filling his lungs with the warm evening air.

As he slowly strolled in the direction of the family's home he couldn't help noticing the beautiful woman who stood with her camera in hand snapping photographs. He had noticed her earlier in the day as she'd taken photographs of the crowd at the rodeo and he'd noticed her during the wedding ceremony and again at the reception. In fact, so in awe of her, he'd spent a good deal of time noticing her, almost forgetting why he was there in the first place.

The exquisite woman was casually dressed in black slacks, a white button-down dress shirt and red Durango cowboy boots. The slacks were cut low against the curve of her round hips and she had the tiniest waist of any woman he had ever seen. Having more leg than torso, she appeared model-tall despite her petite stature. The lengthy appendages gave her the lean, lanky look of a gazelle, and the curvature of her full bustline showed that she clearly had more than a handful. Her flawless complexion was milk chocolate, so rich and decadent that with her distinct features he could easily see her posing on the other side of any camera.

He wasn't quite sure what she was focused on as she stared out in the distance, but with the large telephoto lens and the light that flashed with each snap he was intrigued, curious to discover who she was and what she might be up to.

He casually strolled to her side, his movements so stealthlike that Phaedra didn't notice him until he was standing directly behind her. She jumped, suddenly taken by surprise as the man stepped into her space.

"Good evening," Mason said, a bright smile warming the curvature of his face.

"You scared me," Phaedra gasped, pressing a hand to her chest.

Mason's smile brightened. "My apologies! I didn't mean to frighten you."

"That's what usually happens when you sneak up on a person," she said, her heart still racing.

"I wasn't sneaking," Mason said casually. "You were just distracted. What are you photographing?" he asked as he looked off toward where she'd been staring.

Phaedra was still eyeing him with reservation. When he cut his eye at her and back toward the landscape, a wave of heat suddenly coursed up the length of her spine. He cut his eye at her a second time, a wry smile pulling at his full lips as he waited for her reply.

Phaedra tilted her camera so that he could see the LCD display, depressing the display button so that he could view the images she'd just taken. "Foxes," she said nonchalantly. "There was a family of red foxes scurrying along the fence line."

The man nodded as he met her gaze. "Interesting," he said, his deep voice echoing through the evening air. He extended his hand. "I'm Mason Boudreaux," he said as he wrapped Phaedra's fingers beneath his own.

"Phaedra," she answered, the heat he radiated causing her to take a swift breath. "Phaedra Parrish."

"It's very nice to meet you, Phaedra Parrish."

Phaedra smiled, hoping he wouldn't notice the blush that heated her cheeks. "The pleasure is all mine, Mason Boudreaux."

"You have a very distinct accent," Mason said, noting her deep Southern dialect with its hint of French Creole syntax. "Where are you from in Louisiana?"

"Good ear," she said, smiling sweetly. "New Orleans. Born and raised."

He chuckled softly. "Me, too, although I live in Arizona now."

"I don't hear any accent," Phaedra said, eyeing him with a raised brow.

Mason laughed, shifting into the familiar phonology. "Y'all headed up da house o' ova back da fields?"

Phaedra laughed with him, the warmth of the sound teasing. "So, why Arizona?"

Mason became pensive, hesitating in reflection for a brief moment. "My family was displaced after Hurricane Katrina," he finally said, noting the 2005 category-five storm that had been one of the worst natural disasters on record. "I'd already had a house there and my parents decided to stay when their home was destroyed."

"They didn't want to go back?" Phaedra questioned.

Mason shrugged. "They did and actually, they're back and forth as it suits them. We're still rebuilding the family home, but it's been slow going. That storm really broke their spirits for a bit. And it didn't help that my sister shared its name," he said with slight chuckle. "For whatever reasons, they haven't been in any rush."

Phaedra nodded her understanding. "My mother refused to leave. I was traveling so much for business that she couldn't imagine herself being able to adjust anywhere else. It took everything we both had to repair the damage after the storm, but it was worth it. New Orleans was her home and she was determined to live out the rest of her life where she was happiest. She passed away a few weeks ago," Phaedra said, her voice catching in her throat as she thought about her mother.

"My condolences," Mason said, taking a step in her direction. He drew his hand against the length of her arm. "I'm very sorry for your loss."

Phaedra nodded ever so slightly. His touch was so

powerful that her mind suddenly turned to mush. Phaedra couldn't begin to fathom why she was reacting so intensely. She took a deep breath as she took a step back, suddenly needing to put some distance between them.

Feeling the same thing, Mason crossed his arms over his broad chest, locking his hands beneath his armpits. He hadn't meant to be so forward. There was a brief pause as both pondered how to move past the awkwardness of the moment.

"So, did you enjoy the wedding?" Phaedra asked, wanting to move the conversation in another direction.

"I did. How about you?"

She nodded. "They throw quite a shindig around here."

Mason laughed. "Yes, they do."

"Are you family?" Phaedra asked, curiosity tinting her words.

"By marriage. My sister Katrina is married to Matthew Stallion."

Phaedra's head bobbed against her thin neck a second time. "Your sister, she's pregnant."

"You've met?"

"Not formally. She was with the bride when I took photographs earlier and I noticed."

The man nodded. "This will be her second child, their first baby together. We're all very excited. So, are you related to the Stallions?" Mason asked, having noted a resemblance between Phaedra and the brothers.

There was an awkward pause as Phaedra turned to stare out into the distance. She suddenly wished there was someone with whom she could share her story. Mason appeared to have a compassionate spirit, the breadth of it tempting Phaedra to drop her guard and spill her secret. But Mason's connection to the Stallions made him a highly unlikely ally. After a pause, Phaedra gave a deep sigh and said nothing at all, pretending as though she'd not even heard the question. She lifted her camera, aimed it directly at Mason and snapped the shot, once, twice and then a third time.

Mason found himself smiling, not expecting to suddenly be the center of attention. He shook his head as Phaedra smiled back at him. After a quick moment of silence, Mason spoke. "Well, you look busy, so I'll get out of your way. This was fun, Phaedra Parrish," he concluded, moving as if to leave her side.

Phaedra smiled, meeting his gaze. "Perhaps we'll run into each other again in N'Orleans," she said brightly.

Mason grinned as he lifted his hand in a slight wave. Then as if a lightbulb had gone off in his head, he spun back toward her. "Phaedra, are you doing anything tomorrow?" he questioned.

Phaedra met his gaze. "What did you have in mind?"

"I was thinking breakfast, sightseeing, lunch, maybe even dinner. I haven't had an opportunity to explore Dallas yet, so we can make a day of it if you don't have any plans."

She hesitated only briefly, then nodded, excitement painting her expression. "That sounds like it would be a lot of fun. I'd like that a lot."

"Where are you staying?" Mason asked.

"The Four Seasons."

"I'll pick you up in the morning. Will eight o'clock work for you?"

"I'll be ready at eight," Phaedra answered.

Mason tossed her a quick wink of his eye. "See you tomorrow, Phaedra Parrish!"

Her eyes widening in delight, Phaedra watched as Mason eased his way in the direction of the large homestead. He paused briefly on the front porch to toss her one last wave before he disappeared inside. Lifting her eyes to stare at the moon, Phaedra bubbled with excitement. She suddenly couldn't wait for tomorrow to happen.

Chapter 5

Phaedra was only slightly taken aback when the luxury limousine pulled up in front of the Four Seasons Hotel, the driver beckoning for her attention. She was a bit perturbed when there was no sign of Mason Boudreaux, only instructions for her to be delivered to where he was. Granted, she didn't date often, but when she did she was accustomed to the man actually picking her up. She considered casting one strike against him but hesitated, deciding to at least wait to see where he was waiting for her before she put him on her short list.

When the vehicle pulled into the circular drive of Briscoe Ranch, Phaedra's stomach suddenly did backflips. She hadn't anticipated returning to the Stallion family home so soon and definitely not as the guest of a man she'd just met. Nervous tension creased the lines of her forehead. Since the wedding and the close proximity of the brothers, Phaedra had been in turmoil trying to decide if, when and how she might be able to tell them who she was and what she'd recently learned about her paternity.

As the driver came to a halt in front of the family home, Mason stood at the foot of the stairwell, anxiously awaiting Phaedra's arrival. He'd tossed and turned most of the night thinking about the beautiful woman who'd captured his attention, and he'd been overly anxious to see Phaedra again. He brushed the driver aside as he leaned to open the limo door.

"Good morning," Mason said eagerly, reaching for her hand.

"Good morning to you," Phaedra answered as she stepped out of the vehicle, clasping Mason's hand for support. She gave him a hesitant smile. "I wasn't expecting all this," she said, gesturing at the car, the driver and their surroundings.

Mason laughed warmly, a chuckle rising from deep in his midsection. "Neither was I. But it seems I was expected at the family breakfast this morning and although I tried to get out of it, the family wouldn't let me. So it just made sense for me to send the car for you to join us while my sister lectured me on what I should and shouldn't do on our date today."

Phaedra laughed with him. "Instructions! So you don't date often, I take it."

"Apparently, to hear my sister tell it, not the right way!" the man answered as he cupped his hand beneath her elbow and guided her up the deep steps to the front door.

"Are you sure I won't be intruding?" Phaedra asked, anxiety spinning in the air around her.

Mason shook his head. "Not at all. In fact—" he started just as the front door was thrown open, Marah and Katrina stepping outside to interrupt.

"Good morning!" both women said simultaneously.

"Good morning," Phaedra answered, her eyes widening.

Katrina leaned to give her a warm hug. "Welcome! I'm Katrina Stallion, Mason's sister, and I'm so excited to see you. We didn't get a chance to officially meet yesterday."

"I'm Phaedra," she responded, tossing Mason a quick glance.

The man shook his head. "Be careful," he cautioned, his tone suddenly serious. "If you stand still too long, I'm told, these two will have you married and pregnant before you realize it."

Katrina rolled her eyes skyward. "Ignore my brother, please. Not that it would hurt him to be married and pregnant," she said as she cradled her bulging belly. "We're just excited to see him with a woman our parents would approve of."

Marah laughed. "And Phaedra's not running yet, so there's still hope we haven't scared her off!" she said teasingly.

Phaedra laughed with them. "I don't scare that easily," she quipped as they welcomed her inside the large home.

"That's good," Katrina said, "because we enjoy giving Mason a hard time. But really, we're delighted you could join us for breakfast, although I admit it's not like we gave you much of a choice."

Mason shook his head as he instinctively reached

for Phaedra's hand, clasping her fingers between his own. Her comfort level rose exponentially.

"I appreciate you including me," Phaedra said, squeezing his fingers ever so slightly.

Both Katrina and Marah were grinning broadly as they led the way into the oversize kitchen and family room. There was a crowd of family who greeted them as they made their way inside.

"Let me introduce you to everyone," Marah said as she pulled Phaedra from Mason's grasp. "Everyone, this is Mason's new friend, Phaedra Parrish," she said. "Phaedra, this is the family." Marah gestured around the large oak table. "This is my father, Edward Briscoe, and his wife, Juanita. And that handsome guy right there is my husband, John Stallion."

Phaedra stared as John came to his feet and shook her hand, his smile warm and inviting. Marah continued down the line.

"That woman over there who looks like me, but not as cute, is my twin sister, Marla, her husband, Michael, and that cutie pie in her lap is their son, Michael Jr."

"Hi," the toddler said, eagerly waving both hands in Phaedra's direction.

"Hi," Phaedra said, grinning brightly as she waved back at him. "Aren't you an absolute doll!"

The little boy laughed happily.

Marah chuckled softly. "And this is John's brother Matthew."

"He's mine," Katrina said as she eased her pregnant body into the seat beside her husband, reaching to kiss his lips as she did.

Marah shook her head as she went on. "The big guy

holding that baby girl there is Mark, and his daughter's name is Irene."

Mark lifted a hand and gave Phaedra a slight wave. "Nice to meet you!"

"And you probably remember Mark's wife, Michelle, from the wedding yesterday."

"Everyone calls me Mitch," Michelle said as she adjusted a spit towel over her husband's shoulder, moving him to lift their baby to his shoulder to burp the air from her tummy.

"Hi," Phaedra said softly. "She's a beautiful baby!"

Mark grinned. "Thank you. Takes after her daddy!" he said with a wink of his eye.

Everyone shook their head. Marah continued down the line. "And of course, you remember the bride and groom from yesterday, Luke and Joanne."

"Thank you again for everything," Joanne said as she looped her arm through her new husband's, leaning her head against his shoulder. "You and Hooper did a great job!"

Phaedra nodded. "Hooper's a thrill to work with. I'm glad I was available to assist him."

"Well, he certainly speaks very highly of you," Luke added. "Your reputation preceded you."

"Thank you," Phaedra said.

"And last but definitely not least," Marah concluded, gesturing toward the end of the table, "this is Vanessa Long, a dear family friend, and her baby boy, Vaughan."

"Hey, hey, hey!" Vanessa said, her baby boy clutched awkwardly beneath her arm as she maneuvered a plate in one hand and a bottle in the other.

"I declare," Juanita intoned, moving swiftly to take

the baby from Vanessa's hold. "Girl, you gon' drop that baby holding him like that!"

The family laughed, heads shaking.

"Y'all gon' make my boy soft the way you keep coddling him," Vanessa said. "I need to keep him on his toes. If he bounces once or twice, it'll toughen him up."

Juanita gave the woman a swift slap to the back of her head.

"Ouch, Aunt Juanita!" Vanessa yelled. "That hurt."

"Love tap!" the brothers chorused, everyone breaking out into laughter.

Wide-eyed, Phaedra was suddenly aware of the large hand pressing gently against her lower back, Mason standing comfortably beside her.

"You look overwhelmed!" he said teasingly. "You don't have any siblings, do you?"

She hesitated, her gaze moving along the row of eyes that were staring back at her. Stammering slightly, she shrugged. "I was raised as an only child," she said, "so this is very different for me."

Michelle nodded. "You get used to it," she said. "I was an only child, too."

"So was I," Joanne echoed.

"Please, have a seat," John said, gesturing toward the two empty place settings across from him and Matthew.

"Thank you," Phaedra said as Mason guided her to a chair, pulling it out as she took a seat. He dropped into the chair beside her.

"Ignore this bunch," John said, meeting Phaedra's gaze. "They always get out of hand at family breakfast." His smile was warm and welcoming.

"You all do this often?" Phaedra questioned, her curiosity piqued.

"Every Sunday," John answered. "Once our business went public, Aunt Juanita insisted on it. She felt like we were losing touch with each other."

"It was the only way to get them to relax over a meal," Juanita said, still rocking Vanessa's baby in the cradle of her arms.

"We have two rules for family breakfast," Marah said. "Everyone must show up unless they're out of town. And there is no business discussed. Ever."

"Wow," Phaedra said, impressed. "And everyone always complies?"

John nodded. "It's kept us grounded. Spending a few hours together just being brothers with our families has kept us from taking ourselves too seriously."

"So, where are you from, Phaedra?" Luke asked, resting his chin in his hands as he leaned on the table.

"N'Orleans," Phaedra answered. She twisted a napkin nervously in her lap.

"So are we!" Katrina said excitedly. "Or at least that's where our parents are from. Our father was active army, so we were military brats and traveled around, but the older kids, Mason, Donovan, Kendrick and Kamaya, were all born in New Orleans. I was born in Germany but I can't tell you where the rest of them were born."

Phaedra glanced toward Mason. "How many brothers and sisters do you have?"

Mason laughed. "There are nine of us." He cut an eye at his sister. "Our family meals are quite a bit bigger," he said, his sister nodding her agreement.

Phaedra shook her head and laughed, totally in awe of it all.

Food suddenly appeared out of nowhere, platters of every breakfast item imaginable being passed around the table. Between the food and the fellowship, it was an overabundance of everything. So much so that Phaedra felt as if she were on sensory overload.

She pushed at the eggs on her plate, her stomach still doing flips as she realized she was actually having breakfast with her brothers. Her brothers. John, Matthew, Mark and Luke. The only family she had left. She closed her eyes and took a deep breath and then a second before opening them to find John staring at her curiously. She gave him a slight smile, unnerved by the look he was giving her.

A lanky teenager suddenly entered the room, waving his hand sheepishly at everyone around the table. "Good morning," he said as he reached for an empty plate. Greetings rang back in his direction.

"Collin Broomes, you're late," Katrina chastised, her eyebrows raised as she massaged a hand over her swollen stomach.

"Sorry, Mom," the man-child named Collin answered. "I was helping them muck the stables. It took longer than I expected."

"I hope you took a shower," his mother said, her tone questioning.

Collin rolled his eyes. "Yes, ma'am. That's why I'm late." He moved to an empty chair at the kitchen counter, his plate now filled with bacon and toast.

Matthew chuckled. "I wasn't expecting you to do that before breakfast, son," he said, pride gleaming from his eyes.

The teen nodded. "I know, sir, but I wanted to get it out of the way so that I could ride after breakfast. If that's okay?"

"That's definitely okay," Matthew said. He nodded in Phaedra's direction. "Phaedra, this is our son, Collin. Collin, this is Miss Parrish, your uncle Mason's friend."

Collin tossed his hand hello, his mouth stuffed with food.

"Please, call me Phaedra," she said, waving back.

"Nice to meet you, Miss Phaedra," Collin answered after swallowing. He pointed a finger in Mason's direction, winked at his uncle and grinned.

Mason shook his head as he cut a quick glance at Phaedra.

"Y'all are funny," Phaedra said, lifting her eyes to meet his gaze. She laughed, dropping her manicured hand against his thigh as she leaned her shoulder into his. A jolt of electricity shot through his body and he felt himself quiver from the sensation.

Mason was enjoying every ounce of the moment, conversation flowing with ease. Phaedra didn't seem at all bothered by the family gathering. He understood that this was not at all what she'd been expecting and he was impressed by her sportsmanship, his charming companion seeming very much at ease with their additional breakfast companions.

"So, Phaedra, do you have family in New Orleans?" John suddenly asked.

Phaedra shook her head. "No," she said, her voice catching deep in her throat.

Mason noticed her discomfort at the question. He intervened on her behalf. "Phaedra's mother just passed away a few weeks ago," he said softly.

"Oh, we're so sorry," Marah interjected, everyone turning to stare at the young woman.

"We're very sorry for your loss," Matthew added.

Phaedra nodded, biting down against her bottom lip. She suddenly missed her mother more than she had imagined possible.

"We lost our parents many years ago," John said as he reached a large hand across the table to brush his fingers against the back of her hand. "I know it's not easy."

Phaedra met his stare, holding it ever so briefly, before she pulled her hand from his, clutching her palms together in her lap. She turned to meet Mason's intense gaze, then dropped her stare into her lap with her hands. Tears suddenly pressed hot behind her eyelids. She felt her body begin to shake and she was grateful for the chair beneath her bottom, which kept her from falling to the floor. She swiped at her eyes with the backs of her hands, heat rising to her cheeks as she fought to contain the rise of emotion that was threatening to spill out of her.

"What about your father?" Katrina asked softly. "Is he still alive?"

Everyone in the room was suddenly taken aback when Phaedra suddenly began to sob, her body quivering out of control. Concern wafted thickly around the space.

"Phaedra? What's wrong?" Mason questioned, wrapping an arm around the back of her chair as he leaned in to whisper in her ear. He pressed a napkin to her cheek to stall the flow of saline that rained over her cheeks.

"I'm sorry," Phaedra apologized. "I am so sorry. I

didn't mean…" she gasped, trying to catch her breath as the sobs racked her body.

Mason gently caressed her back, his large hands stroking the width of her shoulders. He was without words, not having a clue what he could say to soothe her. His gaze met John's, the man's stare acknowledging the same sentiment, both lost when it came to a woman's tears.

Juanita was suddenly at her side, a box of tissues in hand. The older woman brushed a warm hand against Phaedra's shoulder. "It's okay, baby. You cry if you want to," she said as she lifted Phaedra's chin with her fingers, brushing the young woman's tears away. She suddenly hesitated, staring deeply. "I declare, child, you look just like Luke when you cry. He gets the ugly face, too," she said, shaking her head.

John laughed. "I was just thinking the same thing," he said, hoping to diffuse the seriousness of the moment. "But your ugly face is definitely prettier than Luke's is," he added.

Luke rolled his eyes. "First off, I don't cry, and when I do, I don't get the ugly face."

"Yeah, you do," Mark chimed in. "And you used to boo-hoo like a baby back in the day. Right up to your sixteenth birthday you'd cry if someone looked at you funny."

Sixteen years old himself, Collin laughed heartily at the thought.

"That is so not true," Luke said.

Phaedra suddenly came to her feet, the napkin in her lap dropping to the floor. She turned her attention to Juanita, who was still trying to console her, something in the woman's stare seeming to acknowledge more than she'd spoken. "Did you by chance know my mother, Miss Juanita? Her name was Arneta Parrish."

Juanita paused, the name spinning through her thoughts. Her eyes suddenly widened, her body tensing. She took a swift breath. "Your mother was Arneta Parrish?"

Phaedra nodded, her gaze still locked with Juanita's.

"Why don't you and I go fix your face?" Juanita said, her hand pressing against Phaedra's arm. "We can talk where it's quiet."

"You know, don't you?" Phaedra questioned suddenly.

"Know what?" John asked curiously, noting the rise of tension that had suddenly filled the space between the two women.

Both turned to stare in his direction. Juanita's gaze moved back to Phaedra, her body starting to shake with nervousness. Phaedra was still staring at John, her gaze moving from his face, to Matthew's, then to Mark and Luke before she locked eyes with him one last time, his stare still questioning.

Phaedra's next words came like lead weights dropping heavily against a wooden floor. "Your father, James David Stallion, was my father, too."

Chapter 6

Phaedra was visibly shaken as she maneuvered her way down the front steps of the family home. Not having a clue how to access the driver and car who'd brought her there, she began to walk as fast as she could, wanting to be as far from all of them as she could possibly manage.

Nothing that had happened in the past ten minutes had been as she'd imagined. After dropping the bomb-shell that she was James Stallion's only daughter, she'd spewed every detail of what she knew, the words spilling out of her mouth like water from a faucet. She couldn't even remember taking a breath as she'd told them all how James and her mother had had an affair resulting in her conception.

Phaedra hadn't known what to expect, but she'd not been at all prepared for the wave of hostility that had suddenly engulfed her. Mark had been the most vocal, insisting there was no way possible for them to share a bloodline. But it was John and his wealth of silence that had been the most unnerving. And when she'd been done, having no other information to share, John had stormed out of the room, brushing past her with a rage that left her feeling completely annihilated, his anguished stare cutting through her like ice.

"She's lying," Mark said as he paced the floor in the home's library. "There is no way she's our sister. We don't have a sister. We can't have a sister."

John stood staring out the large picture window to the fields in the distance. Matthew stared where he stared as Luke drummed his fingers against the oak-topped desk.

"Would Dad have cheated on our mom?" Luke questioned, looking from one brother to the other. He'd only been two years old when his parents had died, and the thought discredited everything he'd ever been told about them.

"No," Mark answered, still pacing, his footsteps heavy against the polished wood floors. "Never!" he said emphatically.

"We really don't know that," Matthew stated, meeting Mark's intense glare. "We would hope not, but anything is possible. Besides, she looks just like us," he noted, turning to face his brothers. "Maybe Dad did step outside of his marriage."

"I know you're not buying that load of horse crap," Mark scoffed. "Are you, John?"

They all turned to John for a reaction, the man still staring out into space. Their big brother hadn't said anything at all since Phaedra's pronouncement. The sting of her words had stunned him into silence and all he had been able to do in that moment was leave the room before he said something he would later regret. He'd left and Matthew, Mark and Luke had followed closely on his heels.

Now he was thinking about their father and their mother, having idolized the two since forever. Their father had always called their mother "Sug," short for "Sugar," his sweet and honey, he used to say. John remembered wanting what his mom and dad had when he grew up and found a wife, their love so magnanimous that he and his brothers use to look on them with awe. He'd wanted to love his woman as hard as he remembered James having loved Irene, and he did, his heart so full for his wife, Marah, that he couldn't ever imagine life without the phenomenal woman.

John also couldn't fathom the thought of being unfaithful to Marah and he couldn't begin to rationalize his father having committed such a crime against his mother. There had been little the couple hadn't shared or done together. John had vivid memories of the two bowling together, camping together and just enjoying the beauty of each other's company. They'd been the perfect complement to each other. His father had been stern and commanding, with only one weakness, his wife. Irene Stallion had been the epitome of virtue, a woman with a huge heart of pure gold. She'd been the most giving person John had ever known, devoting her time and energy to more causes than any of them could ever begin to count. But not once did she sacrifice her children or her family, the Stallion boys always front and center in her mind and her heart.

John smiled as he remembered the many kisses and

hugs and secret touches of affection that had passed between his parents when neither thought anyone was paying attention. The two had shown so much love for each other that to now discover that maybe their relationship hadn't been so perfect was truly challenging his spirit.

Hearing his name being called pulled him back to the moment.

"John, what do you think?" Matthew was questioning, echoing Mark's query.

John turned to face them, his dejected expression causing each of them concern. He shrugged his shoulders, one teardrop escaping past his thick lashes. "I don't know. I don't know anything anymore. Right now Aunt Juanita seems to know more than any one of us ever did."

"Lord, have mercy, this cannot be happening," Juanita whispered loudly as she moved to clear the dishes from the table.

Marah pressed her hand against the woman's arm. "Aunt Juanita, what is this all about?"

Juanita met Marah's gaze. She gently tapped the back of Marah's hand, not saying anything else at all, then continued with the dishes.

"Marah," Edward said, noting his wife's distress. "We'll all talk about it later. Let Juanita be, please."

"I think we need to talk about it now, Daddy," Marah said defiantly, her hand falling to her hip. "Did you see my husband's face? I've never seen John so devastated."

"And Mark was so mad he was ready to spit nails,"

Michelle added as she cradled baby Irene close to her chest. "Mark never gets mad about anything."

Juanita was still shaking her head.

"Is that girl really their sister?" Collin asked, his innocent gaze skating from one adult to the next. "I mean, she does look like them!"

"Collin, why don't you go down to the stables and ride, please," Katrina suggested.

"But, why do—" Collin started.

"Now, Collin," Katrina ordered, her stern tone silencing his question.

Collin mumbled his way out of the room, visibly annoyed that he was always being sent someplace else when it was the adults messing up. When he messed up, it was adult central with all of them coming to toss in two cents. He could sense that things were about to get interesting and he was irritated that he might miss the really good stuff.

"Did you know about this?" Katrina mouthed in her brother's direction, her eyes widened with surprise. Mason had shaken his head at his sister, shrugging in astonishment. It had all happened so fast that he was just as stunned by the turn of events as the rest of them.

As the brothers had left the room in one direction, Phaedra had rushed out in the other. The ensuing commotion from the other women had been a complete distraction. When Mason had turned back to her, Phaedra was gone. Ignoring the questions the women were suddenly hammering him with, he raced to catch up with her.

Outside, Phaedra was doing a run-walk thing up the expansive driveway, her high heels impeding her from breaking out into a full sprint. As he paused at the top of the steps, he stared off in her direction.

Bounding down the steps, Mason raced to catch up to her, calling her name. "Phaedra! Please stop!" he shouted. "Please!"

With Mason suddenly on her heels, Phaedra found herself wishing for a deep hole to drop down into. If there was any way possible for the day to go from bad to worse, having to face Mason Boudreaux had to be it. She picked up her pace, wrapping her arms tightly around her torso. She was still sobbing, her eyes swollen red, and all she wanted was for Mason to go away and not see her in such a state of distress.

Catching up to her, Mason clasped his hand beneath her elbow, gently spinning her around to face him. His heart suddenly cracked, pierced by the pain that shimmered in the woman's dark eyes. Before he realized what he was doing, he pulled her to him and wrapped his arms around her. When Phaedra didn't pull away, allowing herself to give in to the embrace, he tightened his hold as he leaned to whisper in her ear, "I've got you, Phaedra. I've got you. Everything is going to be just fine. I won't let anything hurt you. I promise."

From the family porch Vanessa Long stood staring out at the couple hugging in the middle of the driveway. Her son slept comfortably against her shoulder, the baby oblivious of the excitement around him. Vanessa took a deep breath and then a second as she looked from the papers that Phaedra had dropped, out toward the couple and back again.

Friends with the Stallion sons for as long as any of them could remember, Vanessa was family to them, the only "sister" they had ever known. She'd been best friends with brother Mark first, the two allies on the playground. Vanessa was all tomboy, her daredevil antics rivaling most males and giving each of them a run for his money. For a brief moment, Mark and the woman had been boyfriend and girlfriend, the rest of the family thinking the two would end up head over heels in love with each other. College changed the dynamics of their relationship when Vanessa admitted her predilection for women. Each of the Stallion men had been only slightly disturbed when their family friend had finally come out about her sexuality. But over time they had all found their balance, Vanessa acting as if she were just one of the boys and the brothers treating her so. Then she'd had a baby with the help of a sperm donor and the brothers had each stepped in to be the best uncles baby Vaughan would ever know.

And now Vanessa understood better than anyone that this news had twisted everything the four men had ever believed into a tight knot that might not come undone. Each of the brothers had exalted his father, believing the man had never, in his whole life, done one thing wrong. John, especially, had emulated everything about his father, defining himself as a true alpha male with a rock-solid confidence that radiated from the inside out.

Since his parents' deaths when John was eighteen, every decision he had made for himself and his brothers had been based on the ideologies his father had instilled in him. And each of the brothers had followed suit. Without realizing it, Phaedra had tarnished the gold that was James Stallion, and Vanessa knew that his sons might not ever be the same because of this revelation.

Vanessa turned to face the front door just as John and Matthew stepped out onto the porch. She gave them both a quick smile and a wink as Matthew reached to take baby Vaughan from her arms.

Noticing the papers in her hand, John asked, "Is there anything there that supports what she says?" He stared out to where she stared, Mason and Phaedra still clinging to each other.

"Nothing concrete. I think it's all pure conjecture right now. I can do some digging to see what I can come up with, though," Vanessa said, falling into her private investigator mode.

John nodded. "Do you know where Aunt Juanita disappeared to?"

"She and Mr. Edward took off a few minutes ago. Those women in there were giving her a pretty rough time. He decided they needed to go for a ride before he and Marah got into it."

"My wife can be a little hard on her stepmother."

"Your wife is worried about you guys. So am I."

John cut his eye at Vanessa.

Matthew chuckled softly, nuzzling Vanessa's baby beneath his chin. "Your buddy Mark is about to have a seizure, he's so worked up. Mitch put him on diaper duty for the rest of the day to give him something else to think about."

Vanessa smiled. "Maybe I should add Vaughan to Mark's list, too."

"What list is that?" Mark asked, hearing his name called as he joined them on the porch. Luke followed closely on his heels.

"Your diaper list," Vanessa said with a slight giggle. "I hear you're the go-to man today."

Mark rolled his eyes. "You and my wife need to recognize that I've got skills when it comes to these kids. I'm the go-to man every day!" he said as he dropped into a cushioned rocking chair.

"So, what's next?" Luke asked as he took a seat on the top step and leaned back against the rails. "What are we going to do about her?" He turned to stare up at John.

Mark and Matthew both turned to look at their older brother, anxious for him to answer.

John took a deep breath, filling his lungs with the warm morning air. His gaze was still focused on the young woman standing off in the distance, fighting to regain her composure.

"If what she says is true and she is our sister, then a DNA test will confirm it," John finally said.

Matthew nodded. "I'll call and make the arrangements."

"And then?" Vanessa asked.

John hesitated, his thoughts feeling fractured as they spun through his head. He shrugged. "I haven't gotten that far yet."

Phaedra didn't know why she'd allowed Mason to convince her to go back to the house to continue the conversation with John and his brothers. But she had and now she was sitting in the home's wood-paneled library staring at them as hard as they were staring back at her.

Other than Matthew, who'd been talking into his cell phone, no one had said anything, waiting for what,

Phaedra wasn't sure. The tension in the room was so intense that the young woman imagined they might all self-combust if such a thing were possible.

Seated beside her, Mason had a tight grip on her hand, having promised to not let it, or her, go until she was safe and secure back in her hotel room. She couldn't help wondering what he had to be thinking of her and the drama she'd rained down on them all. So much for their first date, she thought as she stole a glance in his direction, careful not to catch his eye.

Seeming to read her thoughts, Mason drew his hand down the length of her back, an easy caress that helped to calm her nerves. His concern for her well-being was sincere, warming her spirit and affording her a level of comfort she hadn't felt since the last time she'd spent with her mother.

As Matthew seemed to be concluding his telephone call, John came to his feet, reaching for the door. As he pulled it open, Marah, Vanessa and Joanne fell into the entrance, catching themselves before hitting the floor. Mark and Luke both burst out laughing, the chortles gut-deep. Mason grinned, shaking his head. Behind the three women, Katrina stood with a hand pressed over her mouth, her eyes widened, as she tried not to laugh.

John crossed his arms over his chest, eyeing his wife with a raised eyebrow. "I swear," he said, shaking his head. "If I didn't know better I'd declare this whole damn family was crazy."

"Talk about yourself," Vanessa said, her hands gliding down the front of her shirt as if she needed to brush her clothes back into place.

"Sorry," Marah said, embarrassed, her cheeks turning a bright shade of crimson red. "We were…" she started as she shrugged.

"You were being nosy," John finished for her. He extended his arms as Marah stepped into them, easing up on her toes to kiss his cheek.

"Yes, we were," she said.

Luke pointed a finger at his new wife. "Joanne, we leave for our honeymoon in just a few hours. Please do not let these women corrupt you before we do. Please, baby!"

Joanne laughed. "Yes, dear," she said sheepishly.

John chuckled. "I like that. You need to take some pointers from Joanne, Marah. Brush up on your 'yes, dears.' See how nicely she did that? Yes, dear!" he said, mimicking his new sister-in-law.

Marah shook her head. "We just wanted you to know that we'll be in the family room if you need us for anything."

"Anything," Vanessa echoed, pushing a closed fist into her open palm. "We got your back!"

Shaking his head, John closed the door behind them. As he moved back to his seat, he met Phaedra's stare, the woman watching him closely. "They can be a handful sometimes," he said, his full lips bending into a slight smile.

Phaedra smiled back, the bend to her own mouth just as slight.

John cleared his throat as Matthew laid his iPhone on the desktop and sat down, closing the circle of siblings. He leaned forward in his seat, his elbows dropping to his thighs as he rested his chin over his hands.

"Phaedra, first, I want to apologize for anything we may have said or done this morning that may have offended or hurt you. I think I speak for all of us when I say that you really knocked us off guard and I'm embarrassed that we...that I...reacted so horribly."

Phaedra nodded as Mason squeezed her fingers. She continued to listen as John went on.

"I have no doubts that you honestly believe that our father is your father, but I hope that you will understand and not hold it against us if we have some doubts."

"And we have some doubts," Mark chimed in, his body tense as he postured in his seat.

John tossed his brother a look.

Phaedra nodded again. "I was as surprised as you were," she said, her soft voice just shy of being a loud whisper. "And I didn't mean for it to come out the way it did. I just...well..." She paused, looking to Mason and then John as she searched for the words to explain.

John smiled warmly. "I don't think there was any perfect way to say something like that."

Mason shifted in his seat. "Obviously, there is only one way for you all to know the truth," he said, looking from John to Matthew and back.

Matthew nodded. "We've already got that covered," he said. "Phaedra, if you're in agreement, I've arranged for all of us to be DNA-tested tomorrow afternoon. We have a two o'clock appointment at the genetics center in Houston."

"Everyone except me, that is," Luke interjected.

"Everyone except Luke," Matthew acknowledged. "Luke will be in South Africa on his honeymoon."

"But I'm sure if you're related to the rest of these mugs, then you'll be related to me, too," Luke said, winking an eye in Phaedra's direction.

"I wouldn't be so sure of that," Matthew countered.

"We keep telling him that he was found on our doorstep. We don't know where he came from!"

"Ha, ha, ha," Luke said. "I hope you inherited a better sense of humor, Phaedra!"

Phaedra's smile widened. "Thank you," she said.

Mark rolled his eyes. "This is ridiculous," he said. "I don't know why we're wasting the time."

An uneasy quiet fell over the room. Phaedra's gaze skated from one brother to the other, resting on Mark, who was glaring in her direction.

"You know everything I know," she said, her comments directed at Mark. "And after tomorrow we'll know even more. And I understand if you aren't interested in our being family, but if the tests show that we are related, I hope that you'll at least try to get to know me. We might never be friends, but I hope that we won't be enemies."

Mark took a deep breath, brushing his palms against his thighs. He didn't bother to respond as John and Matthew both shook their heads in his direction. "I hear my daughter crying," he said finally. "I need to go change a diaper or something." He stood abruptly and crossed to the other side of the room. He paused in the doorway, his hand clutching tightly to the doorknob. He took a quick glance over his shoulder, his gaze meeting Phaedra's. "I won't be your enemy," he said, his eyes locking with hers.

Phaedra met his stare evenly, tears swelling again in her eyes. She nodded and then he turned and exited the room.

"He'll come around," Luke said softly.

As the others rose to their feet to follow, John extended his hand to shake Mason's. "Thank you," he said. "I appreciate you keeping an eye on our new friend here." He gave the young woman an easy smile.

Mason locked eyes with Phaedra, his own smile widening across his face as she met his gaze and held it. He nodded. "Not to worry. I don't plan to let her out of my sight."

Chapter 7

There was an awkward silence as Mason closed the hotel room door behind them. Phaedra crossed over to the sitting area, dropping her purse to the wooden desk against the wall as she kicked off her high-heeled pumps. Mason stood at the entrance, his gaze following every move. Dropping down into a wingback chair, Phaedra extended her legs in front of her, both hands bearing down against the seat cushion as she twisted her ankles from side to side. She lifted her gaze to study the man who was watching her so intently.

Mason Boudreaux was just shy of being six feet tall. With his hands locked behind his back, his feet shoulder width apart, he was quite the male specimen. His chest was broad, flanked by wide shoulders and thick arms that were indicative of his daily workouts with a very good trainer. His legs were long, the khaki slacks he wore nicely complementing the hard, full, basketball-like curves of his behind. His chocolate-syrup complexion stretched nicely over tight, toned muscles, complementing his closely cropped head of silver-and-black peppered curls. The man was delectable and a seriously pleasant diversion.

She smiled, her lips stretching wide and full over her Colgate smile. "You can come in and have a seat," she said, gesturing for him to join her. "I promise no more hysterical sobbing."

Mason smiled back. "The sobbing didn't bother me."

Phaedra lifted her eyes, a smirk crossing her face.

Mason laughed. "Really, the tears didn't bother me at all," he said as he made his way to the chair beside her and sat down.

"I don't know if I believe you, Mr. Boudreaux, but it's very sweet of you to say so."

He nodded. "I don't know why you wouldn't believe me. I'm usually so convincing," he said teasingly.

Phaedra giggled softly. "I believe that."

Mason laughed with her and then the awkward silence stepped back into the room.

Phaedra closed her eyes for a brief second, wiping her palms across her thighs. Reopening her eyes, she cut her gaze in Mason's direction, the man seeming to be lost in very deep thought.

Phaedra couldn't remember the last time she'd been in such close proximity to such a beautiful man, and Mason Boudreaux was one beautiful specimen of maleness. He exuded strength, his self-confidence, compassionate spirit and obvious integrity like a banner of honor wrapped around him. There was something clearly special about him, and Phaedra found herself wanting to know about everything that made him so.

With her mother dying, then discovering that she had family she knew nothing about, and with one of the biggest photo assignments of her career now on her plate, Phaedra was surprised that she was even thinking about men. But Mason wasn't your average guy next door. Mason Boudreaux was a man a woman couldn't help thinking about.

She lifted her eyes to his. When Mason smiled sweetly, Phaedra smiled back.

"I want to thank you for everything you did for me today," she said softly, "and I want to apologize."

"Apologize for what?"

"For spoiling our first date," Phaedra said, her smile coy.

Mason nodded. "Apology accepted as long as you're willing to give me another chance to impress you," he said with a wry smile back.

Phaedra nodded. "Well, I'm already impressed, but I was thinking that dinner might be a nice idea. My treat, of course, so that I can make up for all the crying."

"I think dinner would be a great idea," Mason answered, meeting her gaze.

And Phaedra couldn't help noticing that there was something she was really starting to like shimmering deep in his eyes.

Collin Broomes rode the large black stallion with an air of confidence. He made two slow laps around the paddock grinning widely from ear to ear. Matthew stood with Mason and John outside the fenced closure, the men all nodding their approval.

"He's a natural," Mason said.

Matthew nodded in agreement. "Collin is exceptionally skilled. I admire the fact that he's allowed himself to learn and he doesn't mind being critiqued. He's come a long way. I am really proud of his maturity."

"We all appreciate the time you've invested in him, Matthew," Mason said. "Collin needed a strong male presence in his life, and you being willing to step up to the plate has been admirable."

Matthew grinned. "I love your sister. How could I not love that big-headed son of hers!" he said with deep chuckle.

John leaned on the fence beside them, taking in the conversation. He didn't say so, but he was as proud of his brother as his brother was proud of the youngster. None of them could have predicted that young Collin stealing Matthew's car months earlier would have ended with Matthew married to the woman of his dreams and about to welcome his own child into the world. It never ceased to amaze him how life could turn on the flip of a dime. He suddenly thought about his own father and Phaedra.

"How was Phaedra when you left her?" John asked, shifting his attention toward Mason.

His friend nodded. "Better. This was a difficult day for her and I don't think she was prepared for it."

"I know we didn't help the situation."

"This isn't easy for any of you," Mason said. "I know Phaedra regrets that it came out the way it did, but ultimately it needed to come out."

Matthew nodded in agreement. "So, tell me," he said curiously. "You and Phaedra seem to have gotten quite close, quite fast. What's up with you two?"

Mason laughed. "What, my sister put you up to asking?"

Matthew laughed with him. "You know she did and you know if I didn't ask I will never hear the end of it."

John's head waved from side to side. "Just to toss in another two cents, Marah made a point of saying you two make a very nice couple."

"Was that before Phaedra dropped her bombshell or after?" Mason questioned.

"Before—" John paused, his eyebrows raised "—and after. Actually, they all really seem to like Phaedra."

Matthew laughed out loud. "It was on the tip of my tongue to say, 'what's not to like?' because the woman is absolutely stunning, but now that she might actually be our sister, that seems kind of weird."

John laughed with him, shaking his head. "You're right! In fact, now that I think about it, if she is our sister, we're going to have to start screening all of her dates. You're lucky, Mason. You've already passed inspection," he joked.

Mason grinned. "I appreciate that!"

"You should," Matthew added, "because I assure you if it turns out that we're related, it's not me or John you'd have to impress. I bet my last dollar Mark is going to be the most overprotective. Phaedra doesn't have a clue what she'll be in for."

John smiled. "I was thinking the same thing. He's playing hard, but Mark is as soft as they come."

"I may be wrong, but I really don't think Phaedra will mind," Mason noted as the three men fell into reflection.

Minutes later Collin lapped the paddock for the umpteenth time and Matthew gestured for the young man's attention. Collin brought the horse to a halt in front of his stepfather and uncles. He leaned forward, his hand gliding down the horse's thick neck. "Isn't he great? He makes it so easy for me to ride."

The horse nuzzled his muzzle against Matthew's hand. "Yeah! He's a good boy. Ride him into the barn. One of the hands will help you unsaddle him. He needs to cool down and be brushed. Then you're going to put him into the stall you mucked earlier. Make sure he has fresh feed before you leave. Understand?"

"Yes, sir."

Collin paused, neither he nor the horse moving.

"Is something wrong, son?" Matthew asked.

"Aren't you going to watch me?"

Matthew shook his head. "No. I trust you'll do what I expect."

Collin raised a questioning eyebrow. "You trust me?"

Matthew smiled. "If I didn't you wouldn't be riding my favorite horse."

With a nod of his head, and a grin as wide as a canyon, Collin galloped the horse toward the barn. John met his brother's gaze, both he and Mason enjoying the moment.

"You're getting pretty good at that father thing," John said, chuckling softly.

Matthew laughed. "I learned from the best, big brother," he said as he bumped shoulders and fists with the man. "I learned from the best."

Juanita was hiding out in the kitchen when John made his way back into the family home. As he stood watching her stir a pot that was bubbling on the stove, he sensed that she was no more interested in having a conversation with him than the man in the moon. But they were going to have to talk because he had questions and she seemed to have all the answers. He called her name, startling her from her thoughts.

"John!" Juanita gasped, pressing a hand to her heart as she spun in his direction.

"I'm sorry, Aunt Juanita. I didn't mean to startle you, but we need to talk."

Juanita sighed. Resting the spoon in her hand on the counter, she bit down against her bottom lip, taking another breath and blowing it out. She gestured for John to follow her to a seat at the counter. "Do you want something to drink, baby?" she asked as he settled himself comfortably on a cushioned stool.

John shook his head no. "But thank you for asking."

Juanita nodded as she took the seat beside him. She'd been regretting this conversation, and no matter how much she wished she could avoid it, she knew John would never consider letting it go. She looked him in the eye as he waited for her to start the conversation.

"Is it true?" John finally asked. "Is it possible that Phaedra is our sister?"

Juanita blew another deep breath. His mother, Irene Stallion, had been her dearest friend in the whole wide world. The two had grown up together, best friends since they'd both been singing in the children's choir of the Baptist church they'd been raised in. They'd gone through every imaginable trial and tribulation with each other, from bad hair to bad boy days. There wasn't a secret Juanita hadn't shared with Irene or Irene with her. And Irene had shared one secret that Juanita had hoped to take to her grave.

John interrupted her thoughts. "I really need the

truth, Aunt Juanita. Was our father unfaithful? Did he cheat on our mother?"

Juanita hesitated, pausing as she took a deep breath. "Yes," she said, meeting his gaze evenly. "But it's not what you think."

"I don't know what to think," John said, cutting to the chase. "But I want facts, not assumptions, so if you can give me that I would really appreciate it. I just need the truth, Aunt Juanita."

Juanita nodded. "You all were just babies. You were five, maybe six. Matthew was three or four, and Mark was just beginning to walk good. That was the first summer that Irene let you boys go to your uncle Joseph's to spend time with Travis."

John nodded. There had been many summers when they'd gone to visit his favorite cousin. He had no memory of that very first summer.

Juanita continued. "Your parents were going through a lot that summer. Your dad had just started his refrigeration repair business. He was working in the factory at nights and running the repair shop during the day. Your mom was also working two jobs and it put a lot of stress on their relationship. The only reason Irene let you boys go was so she could take the time to try to get her marriage back on track."

"And Dad helped her do that by cheating on her?"

"It's more complicated than that. Your mother was lonely. She didn't get to spend a lot of time with James and it was a big issue between them. And then she met this man."

John suddenly slammed his fist against the countertop. Heat flushed his face, rage seeming to rise out of nowhere. Juanita jumped, rattled by the brash display of emotion. John's fists were clenched tight as he processed what he thought she was trying to tell him. Juanita held up both her hands in pause.

"Nothing happened, I swear. Your mother loved your father, but this man could see that she was vulnerable and he preyed on that. The only mistake your mother made was to let this man get into her ear and put doubt into her heart. Your father saw what was happening and it was a nasty blowup, but I swear, nothing ever happened between your mother and that man. Nothing!

"But your father didn't know that. James thought the absolute worst because it looked that way. God knows it looked bad," Juanita said, her head shaking frantically. "James thought he'd lost her. Anyway, that summer your father had gotten the Amana appliance contract to be their regional representative here in Texas and he had to go to New Orleans for a training seminar. He was still thinking that your mother wanted to be with this other man and he just wanted her to be happy, so he left believing that Irene had done him dirty and their marriage was done and finished."

John nodded. "And that's when he met Arneta Parrish?"

"Yes. James was gone for almost two months. When Irene finally realized what had happened, she followed James there and brought him back home. Your father told her about Arneta and it was rough for them for a long time, but they eventually found their way back to each other. No two people have ever loved each other as much as James and Irene loved each other."

"Did he know about Phaedra?"

"No, I don't think so," Juanita said. "If he had, your

father would have acknowledged her and your mother would have supported his decision to do so. James would never have abandoned any child of his. Never! You know better than anyone that your father was not that kind of man."

John's gaze drifted to the view outside the large picture window. He did know. He had always known what kind of man his father was. He had worked all of his life to be at least half that man, emulating the best of who he'd known his dad to be. He was suddenly overcome with emotion, fighting not to break down. Outside, it had begun to rain, dark clouds crying a fine mist of warm water in sympathy.

Relationships were complicated. What John now understood was that whatever challenges his parents might have had to face, and clearly they had gone through some things, when communication broke down between them, they'd been lost. Somehow, though, they'd been able to find their way back to each other and John remembered them only at their very best. All he had ever seen between them had been a wealth of love, that summer of reckoning not even the shimmer of a memory in his mind.

Rising from his seat, John leaned to wrap Juanita in a big bear hug. He kissed her wrinkled cheek, held the gaze she gave him for a brief second, then went in search of his wife. He needed to find sanctuary in what he trusted most, wanting only to hold Marah tight in his arms and to tell her how much she was loved.

Chapter 8

"I owned a hotel-owning company that I just sold to the Stallions."

Phaedra looked slightly confused. "And what exactly is a hotel-owning company?"

Mason smiled. "Mine was an entity that owned, managed, leased or franchised, through various subsidiaries, over four thousand hotels and more than six hundred and fifty thousand guest rooms in one hundred countries and territories around the world."

"Sweet!" Phaedra said. "That's pretty impressive."

Mason shrugged. "It had moments," he said nonchalantly.

The duo had been talking nonstop, the restaurant having closed its doors around them. Bribing the manager, Mason had convinced the man to let them stay, the staff pretending they were not even there. With the exception of their waiter, who would periodically check to see if they needed anything, they hadn't seen anyone else for hours.

Phaedra leaned back in her chair, crossing her legs out in front of her, her hands resting in her lap. "So, what's next for Mason Boudreaux? What's your next business adventure?"

Mason lifted his elbows to the table, resting his chin against the backs of his hands. "I'm not sure. I'm going to take a short sabbatical for a few weeks to wind down and then I'm going to pretend to help your brothers for a few months, although they really don't need my help. Then we'll see. Who knows what might come up?"

Phaedra sighed as she lifted her glass of pinot grigio and took a sip. "My brothers... That sounds so strange," she said, shaking her head.

"I'm sure it's only a matter of time before it will be the most natural thing in the world for you to hear," Mason countered.

"I wish I was as certain as you," she replied with a slight shrug.

Mason shifted his large body in his chair. "So, Ms. Parrish, how long are you planning to be in Dallas?"

"Not long at all actually. I'll stay for the DNA tests tomorrow and then I have to leave for Thailand the day after. I have a photo assignment that I'm contractually obligated to do. I can't get out of it."

"Thailand!" Mason shouted. "You're going to love it! Thailand is beautiful."

"You've been to Thailand?"

Mason nodded. "I've spent a lot of time in Thailand. I used to have a hotel there," he said, smiling, "and I still own some property off the coast of Phuket."

Phaedra looked intrigued. "What kind of property?"

Smiling, Mason leaned forward, moving Phaedra to lean toward him as if he were about to share a deep secret with her. "It's a private island called Koh Rang Yai, one of the most beautiful pieces of property that you could ever experience."

His tone was low and deep and sent a shiver of electricity through Phaedra's core. Phaedra shifted her body back as though she'd been burned. Her eyes widened at the sensation.

"It sounds very special," Phaedra said, her own voice coming in a deep whisper.

Mason smiled. "I'd love to show it to you someday."

"I'd love to see it," Phaedra responded, so lost in the intense look he was giving her that she wasn't sure she'd ever be able to find her way back.

"How about the day after tomorrow?" Mason asked.

"Excuse me?"

"Let me go to Thailand with you and when you're done working I can show you my private island."

Phaedra laughed, tossing her head back against her shoulders. "You're kidding me, right?"

Mason eased himself even closer, dropping a hand against her knee. "I don't kid about things that are important to me," he said.

His seductive tone was just too distracting to be any good for anyone, Phaedra thought suddenly. She took a deep breath, dropped her hand against the back of his and gently pushed his palm away from her leg.

"I am not that kind of girl, Mr. Boudreaux," she said teasingly.

This time Mason laughed, the sound coming from deep in his midsection. He shook his head. "I assure you, Miss Parrish, my intentions are strictly above-board."

Phaedra still eyed him with reservation. "So, why would you want to go to Thailand with me?"

Mason smiled, the look so spectacular that Phaedra found herself holding her breath at the sight of him. When he responded she melted into a puddle of over-stimulated hormones, every nerve ending in her body feeling as if it were about to combust.

"Because you are the most exquisite woman I have ever met and if following you to Thailand will allow me more time to get to know you, then I'm following you to Thailand."

Phaedra paused as she took in his comment. Then she smiled back. "Understand, Mr. Boudreaux, nothing and no one gets in my way when I'm working. So understand there will be no private anything, island or otherwise, between us until after my photo shoot. Is that clear?"

Mason grinned, his head bobbing eagerly. "Crystal."

She nodded. "So, tell me more about your island."

Too fast. Phaedra's words echoed through Mason's thoughts. *You move too fast.* He smiled as he reflected on her. She was obstinate when he'd insisted on them flying his private jet to Bangkok. Phaedra had resisted, reasoning that she had a perfectly good airline ticket courtesy of the company that had hired her to photograph their new line of women's shoes.

It had been Phaedra's suggestion that they shoot in the tropical paradise. Adding her opinion and creative vision to the advertising presentation had helped her beat out fifty other photographers for the job. Her first-class travel expenses had been one of the many perks she'd negotiated for herself and she saw no reason for it to go to waste. But Mason had insisted and she had come kicking, steadfast in her pronouncement that he was moving way too fast for his own good.

Mason smiled as he brushed the backs of his fingers along the profile of her face. She shifted ever so slightly beneath his light touch. He slowly drew back his hand, mindful about not disturbing her rest. She'd been sleeping soundly in the leather seat beside him since they'd stopped to refuel in Tokyo. They'd been in the air for twelve-plus hours and it had taken most of that time for her to finally calm down and relax.

It had been a long and tedious twenty-four hours for them both. Mason had taken Phaedra to Houston for her DNA test, meeting the brothers on-site. And despite their best efforts, just as they had been the day before, John had been reserved, his quiet stance unnerving her. Mark had still been resentful, unreasonably cold and annoyed by the inconvenience of it all. And Matthew had been in full lawyer mode, mindful that there was an appropriate and legal chain of custody to ensure that there would be no tampering with the results.

All of them had to be properly identified and their DNA samples collected with a documented paper trail, and everyone involved, from the specimen collector to the DNA analyst, needed to guarantee that they had no interest in the outcome of the test. It had been an emotional roller coaster for them all.

Mason had held Phaedra's hand through all of it, sensing that she desperately needed a shoulder to lean on. She fought not to show it, but losing her mother and finding brothers while trying to pretend life was normal had shaken her foundation. Mason was determined to keep her upright and moving until she regained her sense of balance. The circumstances of their coming together were well out of the norm, but he was certain that given enough time, normalcy together would be exactly what the two could find. And if he were really moving fast, it was only because he really wanted to know her and he really wanted her to know him.

Mason's laugh was like pure honey, Phaedra thought to herself as she lay with her eyes closed tight, pretending to be asleep. It had to be the thickest, richest, sweetest sound that she'd ever heard. And he enjoyed laughing, easily moving her to laugh with him.

The flight attendant was flirting with him shamelessly, the statuesque woman whispering loudly as she tried to impress him. Phaedra was clearly entertained as Mason struggled to be polite all the while avoiding the overt innuendos the woman was throwing his way. He was cool as a cucumber, but she could hear in his voice that Mason would have liked to be anywhere but in the midst of that conversation with her sitting so close to his side.

She took a deep breath and exhaled loudly, stretching her body against the length of her seat. She sat up as she rubbed her eyes, yawning as if to pull herself from the pretend slumber. Mason smiled excitedly as the flight attendant turned away in a huff, retreating to the plane's galley.

Mason smiled down at Phaedra, his grin spread

from ear to ear. "Hey, sleepyhead! Are you feeling better?"

Phaedra nodded. "Much. I needed a good nap," she answered. "How about you?"

"I feel good. Ready to be back on the ground, though."

"What time is it? Are we close?"

"Yes," Mason said. "In fact, the stewardess was just saying that the pilot will probably be preparing us for landing in the next thirty minutes."

"And what else was she saying?" Phaedra asked, one eyebrow raised as she stared in his direction.

Mason laughed, that syrupy sound caressing her eardrums. "Whatever do you mean?"

"You know exactly what I mean. The way she was tossing her sugar cookies at you, it sounded like she had some serious plans for you two," Phaedra whispered, tossing a glance in the direction of the galley.

"Were you eavesdropping, Ms. Parrish?"

Phaedra nodded. "I most certainly was, and from what I heard, she had plans and you weren't going along willingly."

Mason shook his head, grinning widely. "No, I wasn't," he said, a smirk painted across his expression. "Were you jealous?"

Phaedra laughed. "Do I look like I was jealous?"

"You look a little jealous," he teased.

She leaned closer to him, her smile titillating every nerve ending in his body. "I don't do jealous, Mr. Boudreaux."

Mason leaned in, as well. "Good, because no one has my attention right now except you. You have no reason to be jealous."

Phaedra's smiled brightened as she shook her head. "You are such a man," she said, laughing.

Mason laughed with her. "Woman, you just don't know!"

Chapter 9

Lying in the heart of Southeast Asia, roughly equidistant between India and China, Thailand is distinguished by its breathtaking scenery, featuring spectacular green mountains, white tropical beaches and sparkling blue seas. Within twenty-four hours of her arrival in the capital of Bangkok, Phaedra was so in awe of the culture and her surroundings that she had changed the venue for her shoot, hired new models and was completely immersed in the job she'd been hired to do. She was moving nonstop, barely pausing to rest her eyes.

Like a fly on a wall, Mason disappeared into the background, in awe of her commanding presence. Phaedra knew what she wanted to capture for posterity and what she needed to do to make that happen. Neither the creative director for the project nor the client representative was happy with her, but it was clear that Phaedra was going to give them far more than they'd even begun to imagine.

Mason had taken control that first day, helping Phaedra to acclimate to her new environment. Within hours of arriving he had treated her to a Thai massage at Madara Spa to alleviate the stress of the lengthy trip. Afterward Phaedra had insisted on a quick excursion to Wang Lang Market to try the street food. She'd not been satisfied until she'd had her fill of *muu daeng yan,* a spicy roasted Thai pork with a plateful of springy wheat noodles peppered with chopped scallions. Her meal had been complete when she'd polished off a serving of *kanom krok,* tiny Thai cupcakes baked in a hot metal mold, and more of the crispy tacolike wafers, *kanom buang maprow,* filled with meringue and sweet coconut, than he'd been able to count.

"You have a healthy appetite," Mason said as he passed her a napkin, in awe of the amount of food she'd managed to consume.

"I do like to eat," she said, "and I make no apologies for it."

"I like a woman with a healthy appetite. But as tiny as you are, I'm just trying to figure out where you're putting all that food." Mason laughed.

"That just sounds like another pastry moment to me!" Phaedra said with a wink as she downed her umpteenth wafer dessert.

By the second day Mason was pasted on that wall, an observer in a world that was completely ruled by Phaedra Parrish. The only thing he was allowed to suggest was a ride in a *tuk-tuk,* a rickshaw taxi, that skirted them from one point to another as Phaedra finalized the plans for her assignment.

On day three he followed her to northern Thailand and the Red Karen Village where an indigenous tribe of people known as the Padaung thrived. The Padaung women were renowned for the brass coils they wore around their necks, elongating them for a giraffelike appearance. The extra-long neck was considered a sign of great beauty and wealth and it was thought that such would enable them to better attract a husband.

Women of the tribe identified themselves by their different forms of dress: white robes for single women seeking partners and the brighter colors for married women. Phaedra had been enamored after their guide had explained the coiling process, the brass rings first applied to young girls when they were as young as five years old. As the girls matured, each coil was replaced with a longer coil, the weight of the brass pushing the collarbone down and compressing the rib cage. The illusion of their stretched necks was created by the deformation of their clavicles.

With help from an interpreter, their guide and the permission of a village elder, Phaedra secured the village for her photo shoot. Against the backdrop of a rising sun, the lush greenery of the paddy fields and twelve Padaung girls and teens, Phaedra captured the beauty of high-priced European stilettos, the likes of which had never been done before. When she was finished, no one was more in awe of her than Mason.

Their fourth day in Thailand, after the CEO of that shoe company himself called to express his gratitude for her outstanding work, Phaedra laid her head down on a plush pillow in the luxury suite of their five-star hotel and slept for eighteen straight hours.

* * *

Mason tapped lightly on the door between their adjoining bedrooms. When he got no answer he opened the door slowly and let himself inside. "Rise and shine," Mason said as he tapped the covers atop Phaedra's comatose body. "Time to get up, sleepyhead!"

Phaedra jumped, startled from a very pleasant dream. For a brief moment she had no recollection of where she was or who was talking. Recognition came slowly as Mason stood at the foot of the bed, smiling down at her.

"You're missing all the sunshine," Mason said softly, his hand gently caressing her foot.

Phaedra yawned, stretching her body against the too-comfortable mattress. As she did, the soft covers caressing her skin, she realized that she was naked beneath the sheets. Her eyes widened as she suddenly clutched the covers beneath her chin. "What time is it?" she asked.

"A better question would be, what day is it?" Mason said with a hearty chuckle.

"Have I been asleep that long?"

Mason nodded. "You've missed a whole day. And I've missed you," he added.

Heat suddenly radiated from Phaedra's core, searing everything that made her feminine. She was suddenly feeling very exposed.

"Well," Phaedra said softly, Mason still staring.

He laughed as he winked his eye at her. "I'll give you some privacy," he said. He pointed to a collection of plates resting against the table in the center of the room. "Breakfast is there. It's fresh fruit, coffee, juice, those pastry things you liked and a few traditional Thai dishes. If you want something different just let me know," he said as he moved in the direction of the door.

Phaedra nodded. "So, are we headed to your island today?" she asked, curiosity pulling at her.

Mason shrugged his broad shoulders as he exited the room. "Maybe," he said as he tossed her one last look, "and then again, maybe not!"

"So, what should I wear?" she called after him.

Mason laughed. "I like what you have on now," he answered, the door closing behind him.

Phaedra lifted the edge of the comforter and peered beneath it. What had he seen? Phaedra pondered. She shook her head as she tossed back the covers and slid her body from the bed. She tried to convince herself that he couldn't possibly have seen anything at all.

She paused to savor the assortment of goodies laid out for her to eat, pouring herself a large glass of orange juice and popping a fruit tart into her month, taking note that Mason had started the day nicely.

As she stepped into the glass shower, a warm spray of water raining down over her head and shoulders, she thought about the man, reminiscing about the time they'd shared since meeting at the wedding.

Mason had been solid as a rock. He was intelligent, magnetic, charming and unpretentious. He'd been sweet and caring, sensitive to her needs and most important, he made her laugh. Making her laugh when she couldn't begin to think of anything to even smile about had been the surest way to win her over, and Phaedra was feeling as if she'd struck gold in a landfill. She suddenly realized she was grinning like the Cheshire cat as she rinsed lavender-scented suds from her arms and back. She liked Mason. She liked him a lot and the thought brought more smiles to her face.

Two hours later a private biplane transported them from Bangkok to the coast of Phuket. Mason had teased her, saying that they would be meeting one of his favorite friends, and there she was, moored to the docks at Chalong Bay. His favorite friend was a private sailing yacht, some ninety-one feet long with a striking polished mahogany hull and the most dazzling royal-blue sails that Phaedra had ever seen. The sailboat was named *My Mistress* and she was elegant, a thing of sheer beauty. Reaching for the camera hanging around her neck, Phaedra couldn't resist taking a few photos.

"She's a beauty, isn't she?" Mason said, a hint of pride in his tone.

"Incredible," Phaedra said in agreement. "Is it yours?"

Mason smiled, a slight shrug to his shoulders his only response. He gestured for one of the crew members to come collect their belongings and guided her aboard.

"So, you named her *My Mistress?*" Phaedra questioned, her eyebrows raised.

He laughed heartily. "I was married to my business and when I could sneak away for some necessary R & R, I liked to go sailing. It seemed appropriate at the time."

Phaedra laughed with him. "That's so funny," she said as he led her on a quick tour of the luxury accommodations, a glass of champagne in hand.

Later, when Phaedra stepped out on deck in a pale yellow bikini that complemented the warm tones of her complexion, Mason had to fight not to stare. With her hair piled into a loose chignon atop her head, the woman was stunning, her hourglass figure stirring a low fire deep in him. The sudden rush of excitement threw him completely off guard, the muscles in his body reacting with a mind of their own. Mason guzzled the last of his drink, thinking that he might have to dive ocean-deep to stall the rise of wanting that would give his desire away. He took a seat, dropping swiftly into a deck chair as he crossed a leg over his lap.

As if she could sense his discomfort, Phaedra tossed him a wink, slowly adjusted the line of her bikini bottom, draped a towel beneath her and stretched the length of her frame across the deck chair beside him. She laughed softly as she took a slow sip of her own drink.

Mason didn't miss the crew eyeing her with appreciation and him with envy. Even the captain gave him two thumbs-up as Phaedra made herself comfortable, clearly relishing the cool ocean breeze and the bright midday sun. Before the afternoon was through they set sail, shadowing the Thai shoreline on a course to paradise. As they skimmed the crystal-blue waters in the direction of several islands off the coast of Thailand near the Malaysian sea border, Mason and Phaedra became deadly serious about doing absolutely nothing.

"I could get used to this," Phaedra said, tossing a hand over her eyes to block the sunlight blinding her view. She sat up to stare in Mason's direction.

"Then you should do it as often as you can," Mason answered, opening one eye to meet her gaze.

Phaedra reached for her champagne glass and took another sip. "So, explain to me again why it might take as long as two weeks to get the results back from the DNA tests."

"Two weeks is the maximum amount of time that it should take," Mason responded as he spun his legs off the side of the lounger and sat upright. "According to John, the results should actually be back within the week. But they've requested a full DNA profile be done on all of you, and that takes some time."

"And DNA profiling is where they identify the DNA markers for accurate genetic identity or something like that, right?"

"Yes. Your markers are the short DNA sequences that make up who you are. You get two copies, one inherited from your mother and one inherited from your father. Every person inherits a unique combination of genetic markers from his biological parents. Thus the DNA profile can serve as a permanent biological record of your identity. They have to identify and ensure that you have the same paternal markers they have, which will prove you all have the same father. The techniques and statistical calculations they will use to calculate the probability of your biological relationship just takes time."

"Technology at its finest," Phaedra said facetiously. "What would we do without it?"

"John will call as soon as they know, so stop worrying about it."

"We're on a boat. I don't see too many phone lines floating on that water."

Mason laughed. "John will call," he repeated. "You need to relax."

Phaedra blew a deep sigh.

Mason sat staring at her, the woman struggling not

to meet his gaze. He smiled, the seductive gesture moving Phaedra to squirm ever so slightly in her seat. The electricity between them seemed to give the boat more speed as it glided through the glassy waters.

"Don't look at me like that," she said suddenly.

"Like what?"

"Like the way you're looking at me. I feel naked."

He laughed again. "I'm looking at you because you're so beautiful and if I'm honest, I wish you were naked," he said casually.

"Aren't you the pervert?" Phaedra responded as she rolled her eyes.

"Come here," Mason said, a crooked index finger waving her toward him.

"What?"

"Come here," Mason said, his voice dropping low, the seductive tone like a sweet caress against Phaedra's ears.

Intrigued, Phaedra rose from her seat, the string bikini she wore, more string than bikini, looking like wet paint against her toned form. As she moved to his side, Mason lifted his legs to straddle the cushioned lounger he was seated on. He patted the seat between his legs.

"Sit here," he said, holding up a hand to guide her down to the seat.

Turning her back to his chest Phaedra sat down between his legs, stretching the length of her own legs outward. Mason wrapped his arms around her waist and pulled her against him, nestling the round of her buttocks against his pelvis. Phaedra inhaled swiftly, the warmth of his touch startling. He gently pressed his fingers against the back of her neck, slowly kneading the soft flesh beneath his fingertips.

Without realizing it Phaedra gave in to the sensations sweeping through her body. She was loving the feeling of sitting so close to him. She dropped her chin down toward her chest and leaned forward to allow him better access to the muscles that had tightened through her neck and across her shoulder blades. Heat radiated from his palms, pleasure burning deep into her core.

Mason loved how his touch was affecting her. Phaedra's legs relaxed, then flexed, her body beginning to quiver. Her hands tightened as she clutched them in tight fists. Her eyes were closed and her breathing started to come in short gasps as she subconsciously licked her lips. When she moaned, the sound like a soft purr, he chuckled softly, causing Phaedra to jump out of the reverie. Taken aback, she leaped from her seat, skirting far from Mason's touch.

"What's wrong?" Mason asked, his grin disarming her sensibilities.

"You…you…you shouldn't have been doing that!" Phaedra stammered, her breathing heavy.

"Doing what?"

"That… What you were doing!"

He laughed, his head waving. "I was only giving you a massage."

"That wasn't just a massage."

"But you liked what I was doing and you liked how I was doing it," he said matter-of-factly.

Heat flushed her face and her complexion tinted a deep red at the truth of his statement. She had enjoyed it and if she were honest she had wanted him to do much more. "That's beside the point," Phaedra said, crossing her arms over her chest.

Mason laughed loudly. "Fine," he said, "instead of giving you a massage myself I'll call for someone on the island to come ease the tension out of your muscles. Will that be better?"

Phaedra rolled her eyes. "You think you're cute."

Mason smiled brightly. "Yes, I do!"

Two days later Phaedra couldn't imagine their time together getting any better. The captain had guided the boat into a channel cradled between the islands. They were wined and dined on deck, the tantalizing meals unending. Mason's personal chef overwhelmed them with fresh fish chowders, amazing salads, vine-ripened fruits and sumptuous Thai cuisine. When they weren't dozing deckside, falling asleep to the sound of small waves slapping against the hull, they were snorkeling above exquisite coral gardens. They awoke to the beauty of the rising sun in the mornings, and in the evenings, the sunsets seemed spiritual, each one more soothing and poignant than the last.

Through it all Mason remained the perfect gentleman. He had called in a professional masseuse for them both, the woman arriving by dinghy to join the crew. More times than not she caught him staring, the looks he gave her like daggers of piercing heat. There was no mistaking the waves of desire that danced between the two of them. But Phaedra wasn't ready to move their newfound friendship in a more intimate direction. And despite having the best spa services at their disposal, Phaedra couldn't stop herself from thinking of Mason and the way he had touched her, wishing him to do it all over again.

Phaedra couldn't begin to imagine why she was so restless. She and Mason had spent most of the night deckside in deep conversation, sharing everything they could possibly think to share with each other. She'd heard stories about his family and had talked about her relationship with her mother. They'd confided details of her first kiss, his first sexual encounter, their most embarrassing moments, biggest fears and greatest hopes. They had discovered things about each other that no one else knew, and no topic had been off-limits.

When they'd parted ways, she going to her cabin and he to his, both had wished for a few more minutes, neither wanting to let the other go. Then Phaedra had tossed and turned in her bed, unable to explain the wealth of emotion she was feeling. She blew a deep sigh as she sat upright in the bed, tossing her legs over the side.

The heat from the morning sun had awakened her, making her cabin too warm to sleep in. Rising, she slipped into a one-piece bathing suit and wrapped a brightly colored sarong around her hips, then maneuvered herself topside to look around. Mason was already sitting comfortably beneath the bright blue sky, a glass of fresh-squeezed juice in his hand.

"Good morning," the man said.

"Good morning."

"Did you sleep well?"

Phaedra nodded. "I slept okay, not great," she said as she reached for the glass of juice he was passing to her.

He nodded his understanding, knowing full well what she was describing. He hadn't slept well, either, the night spent thinking of her and nothing else.

She took the seat beside him. "So, what's on the agenda today?" she asked casually, both hands wrapped around the crystal glass. "Will I get to see that island of yours sometime soon?"

Mason nodded as he met her stare. He pointed a finger to the landscape behind her back. Turning to stare past the boat's stern, Phaedra eyed the white-sand beach that ran along the side of the boat, kissing the dazzling turquoise channel beneath them. A dense jungle fronted the entire length of the beach, a formidable barrier to the naked eye. The place seemed divinely empty, unspoiled and promising a peaceful quiet to anyone willing to brave the terrain.

Jutting out of the water on stilts were four thatched-roof, overwater bungalows, each featuring a glass-bottomed floor that allowed stunning views of the marine life below. With private decks, each with steps down into the lagoon for easy access to the water, the simplicity of the accommodations was breathtaking.

A lone figure dotted the beachside, a fisherman who waved excitedly in their direction. In the waters that surrounded the land, clouds of tropical fish shimmered and danced in erratic synchronized displays. Puffer fish, angelfish and sea urchins hid in coral passages. A manta ray glided lazily along the bottom as he headed out to sea. Phaedra stole a quick glance toward Mason, a look of sheer enchantment crossing her face.

"Welcome to my home," Mason said as he moved against her back, wrapping his arms around her torso and nuzzling his face into her hair.

Taking a deep breath of warm ocean air, Phaedra relaxed against him, allowing herself to savor the sweet sensation of being in his arms.

Chapter 10

They were having dinner in Phuket, an outrigger canoe scheduled to pick them up and carry them to their destination. After their arrival on the island, Mason had given Phaedra a quick tour of her hut before disappearing to his own. Knowing that the beautiful woman had only bought casual clothes for her trip, he arranged for a selection of formal clothing to be delivered to her room.

Phaedra had sent him a text message when the rack of garments had arrived, her appreciation evident in the words on his smartphone screen. Mason smiled, moving to the window to stare toward her hut. Phaedra stood in the open entrance of her own space and waved in gratitude. The two paused, staring intently at each other. Then Phaedra moved back inside, disappearing to get dressed.

Dropping down onto the king-size bed in his room,

Mason closed his eyes and took a deep breath. There was something brewing between him and Phaedra, like nothing he had ever experienced before. It was exciting and special and it had seeped deep beneath his skin to spread like wildfire into his system. It was something he'd been searching for since forever, never imagining that it would feel quite as magnanimous as this.

An hour or so later Mason waited on the dock as Phaedra made her way toward him. She'd chosen a simple Monique Lhuillier black lace cocktail dress with mile-high Christian Louboutin stilettos. Her lush curls had been straightened, hanging down to her shoulders. The entire ensemble flattered the petite lines of her frame, the strapless styling absolutely stunning on her. Mason couldn't find words.

"Is this okay?" Phaedra asked, doing a pivot turn in front of him.

Mason smiled, nodding sheepishly. "Wow," he said, his gaze skirting the lines of her body, racing from the tip of her head to the bottoms of her feet. "Wow!"

Phaedra smiled back. "I'll take that as a yes."

"Yes," Mason said. "You look amazing!"

Phaedra glanced toward the skipper of the canoe, who was waiting patiently for them to board.

Mason followed her gaze. "Your chariot awaits, madame!"

She nodded as she eased around him, stepping gently to keep from falling into the water. As she stepped into his space, Mason inhaled the scent of her perfume, a light floral fragrance wafting beneath his nose. Before he realized what he was doing, he clutched her arm, pulling her to him. He hesitated for only a moment, Phaedra meeting his intense stare with a look of her own. Her breath caught deep in her chest, her heart racing unexpectedly.

Without a second thought Mason leaned in to kiss her, allowing his lips to lightly graze hers. His breath was hot with wanting, his full lips quivering in anticipation. He pulled away and stared into her eyes a second time and then he dropped his mouth to hers, meeting Phaedra's lips in a deep, soul-searing kiss.

Time seemed to come to a standstill. Phaedra felt as if the world had rotated her into the stratosphere, everything spinning around her. Mason held her tightly, his hands burning hot against the bare skin of her arms and shoulders. His body melded tight to hers and both were in awe of the sensations, feeling as if they were melting—one into the other. When he finally pulled back he knew beyond any doubt that he had absolutely fallen in love with Phaedra and Phaedra was falling in love with him.

They had dinner reservations at Da Maurizio Bar Ristorante, located on Patong Beach. Da Maurizio was considered the finest contemporary Italian restaurant in the south of Thailand and had won numerous awards. With the granite boulder-strewn beach below the alfresco dining room, it counted Mother Nature as part of the decor. The white linen tablecloths, colorful bar and brick floors served to complement the classic Italian styling. It was clearly one of the most beautiful dining venues in Phuket, stylish, impressive, memorable and unpretentious.

A light Italian ballad played in the background as Mason and Phaedra stepped inside, her hand entwined with his, both still floating from the kiss they'd shared.

The hostess greeted him by name, quickly escorting them to one of their best tables, and the impeccably clad waitstaff hovered at the ready to do his bidding. For a brief moment Phaedra regretted not bringing her camera to capture the eclectic mix of diners who had come from all over the globe to enjoy the constant background flow of the Andaman Sea, which helped the restaurant's atmosphere remain true to Thailand's laid-back reputation.

Mason ordered dinner for them, starting with a gourmet appetizer treat of foie gras and candied walnuts atop cubed green apples on a crisp homemade raisin bread and port wine reduction and fresh al dente fettuccine with marinated and lightly seared yellowfin tuna, capers, Gaeta olives and anchovies. They had just begun their meal when Phaedra saw the woman enter the room.

Phaedra saw her before Mason did, the stunning beauty catching the attention of everyone in the room. She was tall and slender, her figure more androgynous than feminine, as she sported a leopard-print jumpsuit with matching high-heeled shoes. Her jet-black hair was closely cropped around the back, and she had long sweeping bangs streaked with vibrant gold highlights that complemented her distinctive Asian features. With the exception of her bright red lips, her makeup was subtle, impeccably applied.

Phaedra took notice of her just as the woman took notice of Mason. There was no missing the woman's excitement that shimmered out of her eyes. The man who'd stepped in behind her noticed it as well, quietly admonishing her to calm down. Phaedra pressed a napkin to her mouth as the woman rushed toward their table, her companion following closely on her heels.

"Mason Boudreaux," the older man said, calling for Mason's attention.

Mason looked up in surprise. "Daniel, hello," he said, rising from his seat to shake the man's hand. "What a wonderful surprise."

"We did not know you were back in Thailand," the man said.

"You should have called, Mason," his female companion said, moving to wrap Mason in a deep hug. She kept her arms wrapped around his waist as if she were afraid to let go.

Mason smiled politely. "It's good to see you, Mali," he said.

Extricating himself from the woman's grasp, he moved to Phaedra's side, taking her hand in his. "Allow me to introduce you to my dear friend. Phaedra, this is Daniel Kasam and his daughter, Mali Kasam. Daniel is one of the most respected politicians here in Thailand. Daniel, Mali, this is my friend, and my traveling companion, Phaedra Parrish."

The man named Daniel gave Phaedra a wide smile. "It's a pleasure to meet you, Miss Parrish. Mason and I have been good friends for many, many years."

"Please, call me Phaedra. It's nice to meet you both, as well," Phaedra responded as Daniel took her hand and pressed a kiss to the back of her fingers.

His daughter eyed her from head to toe, her expression blank. When Mason dropped his hand to Phaedra's shoulder, gently caressing her warm flesh, the woman's face twisted in a harsh snarl. Mali glared and Phaedra held the harsh stare, hardly intimidated.

"How long will you be in town?" Daniel asked, appearing to not see his daughter's behavior.

"Just a few more days," Mason answered. "Phaedra has business back in the United States, so we'll be heading back home by the end of the week."

"Well, we must have dinner together before you leave. Are you two free tomorrow night?" the other man asked, looking from Mason to Phaedra and back.

Phaedra glanced up to see Mason eyeing Mali with reservation. He sensed her staring at him and tossed her a quick look. Taking a deep breath, he smiled sweetly, giving her a quick wink.

"We'd love to," he said as he gently squeezed Phaedra's shoulder.

"Wonderful!" Daniel said. "Then we'll catch up with each other tomorrow."

"We both look forward to it," Mason concluded, moving to shake the man's hand one last time.

As her father turned away, Mali moved herself against Mason, clutching the front of his suit jacket as she pressed her body to his. She leaned to kiss his closed mouth, moving her lips earnestly over his. "I've missed you, Mason," she whispered seductively. Before Mason could answer, Daniel called his daughter's name, admonishing the woman in their native Siamese language.

Mali huffed in annoyance as she stepped away. "Tomorrow," she said, tossing the man one last wink and as she turned to follow her father, she gave Phaedra one last glare.

When both were out of earshot, Phaedra shook her head. "Well, well, well," she said, bemusement shimmering across her face. "You didn't tell me about your ex," she said.

"Mali is not my ex," he said with a deep chuckle. "There has never been anything between me and her."

Phaedra tossed Mali one last look as the woman and her father joined a group gathered in the private dining room. "Well," she said, lifting her gaze back to his, "someone clearly forgot to tell her that!"

Phaedra hadn't missed Mali's blatant interest in the handsome bachelor. What she didn't know was that Mali had been vying for Mason's attention for as long as he could remember, but her brash behavior and brazen antics had been a complete turnoff for him. Despite the woman's obvious overtures, Mason only had eyes for Phaedra, clearly intoxicated with her, and he told her so. Phaedra was the sweetest addiction that had ever consumed him, and his only interest was the magnetic attraction between them. Shaking his head, Mason changed the subject.

The rest of their meal was uneventful. After a main course of rosemary lamb chops sitting on a mint salsa verde and lemon yogurt with herbed couscous, they finished their dinner with a decadent tiramisu. Sated beyond reason, Phaedra couldn't imagine them having a better time.

"Have I thanked you yet? Our time here in Thailand has been absolutely amazing," she said as she reached for his hand, drawing her fingers against his open palm.

"Many times, but you don't have to keep thanking me, Phaedra. I really haven't done anything."

Phaedra shook her head. "But you have and I think that couples sometimes forget to acknowledge each other and show their appreciation for what each does. I don't want that to happen with us."

Mason smiled. "And are we a couple?"

Phaedra was suddenly overwhelmed by the look he was giving her. His stare was eager and searching. She felt as if she were falling headfirst into his gaze, able to lose herself completely if she were willing to let go. She was grateful for the distraction when the waiter appeared at the table with the dinner bill.

On the ride back to the island, Mason took off his suit jacket, wrapping it around her shoulders to shield her from the cool night air. Phaedra rested her head against his shoulder, reveling in the soft light of a full moon and the dark sky littered with bright stars.

"This has been wonderful," Phaedra said, her voice floating through the darkness. She spun around, wrapping her arms around his waist as she rested her cheek against his broad chest.

As Mason leaned to kiss her forehead, there was nothing else he needed to say, everything about the moment agreeing with her.

Chapter 11

Mason had kissed her one last time before wishing her a good night. Phaedra had stood in the doorway of her bungalow, watching as he made his exit, returning to his own room. For a split second she'd thought about calling him back to her and then she didn't.

She couldn't help questioning where the two of them might be going with their relationship, a discussion they had yet to have. She knew he was ready for marriage and children and family, anxious for that next phase in his life. Yet, he knew that she'd never given those thoughts much consideration, her career taking precedence over all else. They had talked in generalizations, but now the discussion of how that affected the two of them together needed to be shared. Because Phaedra did feel like the other half of a couple, but when he'd asked, she hadn't been ready to say yes.

If they were moving too fast, she didn't want to be

the one initiating the race. Mason seemed content to let her set the pace, and Phaedra didn't want to rush if it were at all possible for the two of them to be thinking about forever with each other. Because Phaedra found herself thinking about forever with Mason Boudreaux.

Phaedra stepped out of her clothes, tossing her dress over a chair and kicking her shoes into a corner. She dropped down against the feathered mattress, her hands resting against her upper thighs. Music played softly from speakers in the wall, a slow, erotic tune with a deep, sultry base. The song seemed to have a certain power over her, the seductive lyrics and entrancing beat making her want to dance and make love all at the same time. Her body tingled, heat beginning to creep from her southern quadrant as she swayed from side to side.

Outside, a loud splash of water drew her attention. Phaedra moved to the open window to peer outside. Beneath the glow of moonlight she couldn't miss Mason, the man having dropped down into the lagoon for a late night swim. The water around him glistened, shimmering from the reflection of the light above as his muscular body floated atop the watery bed. Intoxicated by the music and wanting more from the man who had her full attention, Phaedra stepped out of her panties, took a deep breath, then headed out the door.

Mason was taken by surprise when Phaedra stepped out onto the edge of the dock. She was as naked as the day she'd been born. He'd been swimming laps between their two bungalows and when he saw her he stopped midstroke and began to tread water, taking a moment to appreciate the gorgeous sight as she posed seductively in front of him.

Phaedra loved the cool sensation of fresh air on her

exposed breasts, the dark chocolate areolas surrounding candy-hard nipples. A breeze blew like a fine mist between her legs, moisture beginning to pool between her creases. But the intense sensations were nothing compared to what she felt when she saw the look on Mason's face, the man looking as if he were experiencing the single greatest moment of his life.

Neither spoke, but there was no denying the rise of wanting that was spiraling between them. Even beneath the blanket of cool water, Mason's muscles tightened, blood surging with a vengeance below his waist. His erection stretched full and hard, feeling as if it might explode if he even thought about the woman. He bit down against his bottom lip, wanting to still the rise of nature between his muscular legs.

Holding on to the wooden ladder that dropped into the natural pool, Phaedra slowly eased her body into the water to join him. The chill of the moisture did nothing to ease the heat that was consuming her. Phaedra wanted him. She wanted him more than she had ever wanted any man in her life, and if that made her fast, she thought, then she was past ready to set a new record.

Mason swam toward her as she moved into his arms. He wrapped one arm around her waist as he maneuvered her against the dock where he could grab on to the structure with his other hand. The light floral scent of her perfume surrounded him, blending with the sweet ocean air. He seized her mouth hungrily, barely daring to believe that this moment had finally arrived. His mouth clung to hers, and he felt her tongue meet his own, the two dancing deep in her mouth. Tasting the sweet fullness of her lips, Mason couldn't help biting down on her bottom lip, then nibbling on her top lip. Their kiss was heated and intense, just a semblance of the hunger they had for each other.

Yearning for more, Mason braced himself against the wooden steps as Phaedra wrapped her legs around his waist. She pressed her pelvis against the length of his manhood and it took everything he had not to explode from the connection. His mouth did a nosedive and landed smack on her nipple, greedily sucking and tugging and pulling at her with his teeth and lips. Phaedra let out a loud gasp, the sound resonating between a moan and a scream. It was almost too much for her to bear as his hands followed his mouth, kneading and pulling at the fleshy tissue.

The duo dropped beneath the water. They both held their breaths, lost in the sensations of his touch and hers as they clung to each other. It was eerily quiet, their beating hearts all either of them could hear above the swell of the ocean. When they resurfaced, the sounds of their desire rose to a crescendo that echoed through the night air.

"We need protection," Mason whispered, thinking of a prophylactic before the moment consumed them and he wouldn't be able to think of anything except the pleasure the two were intent on giving each other.

Phaedra nodded as he lifted her from the water, setting her easily atop the wooden platform. He lifted his body from the water, reached for her hand and led her back inside his bungalow. Inside, he snatched the bed's coverings and tossed them to the floor. Lifting her into his arms, Mason kissed her again as he laid her gently down against the mattress. His swimming trunks tented eagerly between them.

"Do you really want me, Phaedra?" he questioned, stopping to stare down at her.

Phaedra responded by pulling him back to her, her mouth dancing like silk against his. Inhaling her scent, Mason ran the tip of his nose up and down the side of Phaedra's neck, then did the same with his lips and then his fingers. Goose bumps rose against Phaedra's damp skin as he teased her feminine spirit. His kisses became more and more intense until he was gently sucking on her neck, his teeth lightly biting her soft, pliant throat until tiny little marks began to rise against her flesh. Beyond any doubt he knew that she was his, and he couldn't help wanting to mark her and stake his territory.

Beneath him Phaedra was slowly grinding her pelvis against the rigid hardness between his legs. She reached her hands around his torso and raked her nails down the length of his back. It was the sweetest pleasure and most delightful pain. Snaking her way down into his wet swim trunks, she pushed the garment off the firm globes of his behind, squeezing and kneading the taut flesh.

Her touch was too much for him to handle. Every muscle ached with wanting for her. Mason lifted his body from hers and moved to the dresser and the leather toiletry bag that rested atop the marble surface. Pulling a condom from the side pocket of the leather case, Mason tore the cellophane pack open with his teeth, then rolled the rubber over his protruding member. Dropping his body back down against hers, Mason drew a slow path against her skin as he kissed her stomach, sinking his tongue into her belly button.

Phaedra pulled her fingers across his cropped hair, the silky curls tickling her skin.

She was grinding unabashedly as he kissed his way back to her breasts, suckling one and then the other, then biting the skin beneath her chin, until he reached her mouth and kissed her, his tongue darting back and forth with hers.

Mason grabbed one of her hands and then the other, pulling her arms high above her head. Phaedra gasped as he eased himself between her thighs, using his knees and body to pry her legs open. He held her captive with his gaze as he lifted himself ever so slightly to stare down at her. She called his name, the echo of it caressing his spirit.

"Mason!"

Nodding, Mason pressed his mouth back to hers and whispered against her lips, "I love you, Phaedra."

Tears glistened in Phaedra's eyes. The words were there, caught deep in the wealth of emotion that filled her spirit. She loved him, too. More than she'd ever imagined possible. She choked back sobs that obstructed her words. She loved him and every fiber of her being wanted to tell him so. Instead she responded with her tongue, voicing it in her kiss and touch and the easy caress of her body against his. Mason slowly eased the length of himself into her. As he pushed himself forward, moisture dripped past his thick lashes, mingling with the tears that rained down Phaedra's cheeks. The moment was surreal, the magnitude of the experience sweeping sensations through them both as neither had ever experienced before. It was more than Phaedra could ever have imagined, and with her arms still captured above her head, Mason's mouth locked with hers, his breath kissing her breath, Phaedra lifted her hips and welcomed him home.

Mason couldn't remember when they'd fallen asleep. They'd made love over and over again, their desire for each other almost insatiable. There'd been no place in the room that he hadn't taken her, their sexual aerobics moving from the bed to the floor, against each of the four walls and back to the bed again. He wouldn't have thought it at all possible, but he was still hard, desire still lengthening his manhood in anticipation. He shivered, his muscles quivering with want.

Phaedra slumbered comfortably beside him, her back curled against his body. Heat wafted off her skin, igniting a flame deep in his core. He pressed himself against her, savoring the sensation of her buttocks cradled against his crotch. He hardened even more, his male member twitching as he drew a light hand down the length of her arm, his palm coming to rest against her hip. He was in awe of just how beautiful she was, as exquisite inside as she was on the outside. As if she could read his thoughts, Phaedra snuggled closer to him, wiggling her body from the waist as she pressed her bottom closer against him.

Reaching across her body, Mason cupped her breasts in the palm of hand. They were absolutely divine, he thought as he gently kneaded one and then the other between his fingers. Phaedra stirred again, her body squirming against his. She turned in his arms, rolling onto her back, and he lowered his lips to her nipple, his tongue slathering one and then the other. He savored the sensation of them hardening in his mouth.

Phaedra moaned softly, leaving sleep behind as she

woke to the moment. She could get used to wakening to such delicious sensations sweeping through her body, she thought, and Mason was becoming an expert at eliciting the most enchanting vibrations from her. She clasped her thighs tightly together with desire from his ministrations.

Mason chuckled softly as he whispered good morning, and all she could do was moan in response. He slid a large hand between her legs, gently inserting his middle finger into her wet folds. Phaedra shuddered with ecstasy, his touch causing her to swoon. She wrapped her arms around him, a smile pulling at her lips as she embraced him tightly.

Moving up her body, Mason nuzzled and kissed her throat as she threw her head back against the pillow, sighing and moaning with delight. His continued strumming the spot between her legs, expertly playing her like a bass player with his instrument. He played notes on her labia, his fingertips dancing against her sweet spot until she was senseless with ecstasy. Sensing that her climax was imminent, Mason drove his fingers deep inside her while still stroking her with his thumb. He grinned, relishing the expression on her face as Phaedra exploded into a screaming orgasm that left her breathless and squirming.

There was vulnerability in her eyes when she opened them to meet his gaze, her breathing still coming in short gasps. Mason smiled as he shifted his body atop hers, his nakedness kissing her nakedness. He brushed his lips against her lips, kissing her softly, leading a damp trail of gentle kisses all along her cheeks, at the tip of her nose and across her eyes.

Their gazes locked, and both felt something stir

deep within them. Mason sought her mouth a second time, his hands moving furiously over the length of her body. His breathing became labored as his excitement increased, his erection so hard that he felt as if he were about to explode without being touched. But the moment wasn't about him, he thought, his desire to bring her pleasure outweighing the need for his own release.

He kissed a trail down the length of her body, back to her neck, across her stomach and downward as he sought out the rich scent of her femaleness. He then pushed her legs up and out, exposing her most private place. Phaedra's eyes were widened in anticipation. She inhaled swiftly as he gently slid his tongue into that soft, sweet wetness and then she moaned loudly with pure, unadulterated lust. She clamped her hands down against the back of Mason's head, willing him to never stop the heavenly sensations he was creating.

Mason was nearly on the edge himself, knowing how much pleasure he was bringing the stunning woman. He slid his fingers inside her and she moaned his name, a soft mantra chanted over and over again. He fingered her slowly, matching each thrust with the flick of his tongue across her swollen love button. Phaedra's hips bucked against his mouth and hand as he increased the firmness of his touch. He stroked her, feeling her open up more and more with each pass of his fingers. Phaedra's moans were reaching a frenzy as she clutched her breasts. In that moment, nothing existed but the two of them together and as Phaedra exploded in orgasm Mason's own release surged between his legs.

They lay together panting, both stunned by the intensity of what was happening between them. Mason lay with his head cradled against her abdomen, Phaedra gently caressing the side of his face.

"You're incredible," Phaedra whispered, leaning up on one elbow to look into his eyes. "I didn't think it could get any more amazing with us."

Mason pressed a kiss against her belly button. "Baby, we're just getting started. We haven't even tapped into amazing yet!"

Chapter 12

Phaedra had no idea of the time. The sun had risen, the day had passed and she'd been oblivious, focused only on Mason and what they were sharing between them. For most of the afternoon all they'd done was make love, talk, talk and make love. She couldn't remember being so happy and only briefly did she think that such might never have been possible if her mother had not been taken from her life when she had.

Phaedra would have loved to still be in bed with Mason, the two focused solely on each other and nothing else. Instead they were headed to Cape Yamu in Phuket to have an early dinner with the Kasam family. She stole a glance toward Mason, who was lost in his own thoughts as the driver of the private car they were in maneuvered his way through the streets of Phuket.

The man was absolutely stunning, she thought, a smile rising to her face. His attire was dress casual, black slacks, black blazer and a white dress shirt opened at the collar. He was impressive the silk suit fitting him to perfection. Phaedra had chosen a halter jumpsuit from the collection of clothing Mason had made available to her, the red linen complementing the warm brown tones of her complexion. Side by side they made a beautiful couple. As if he were reading her mind and thinking the same thing, Mason squeezed her thigh, smiling sweetly at her.

"Are you sure you don't mind doing this?" Mason asked once again.

Phaedra gave him a smile back. "Of course not. Why would I?"

"Mali," he said, his eyebrows arched knowingly.

Phaedra laughed. "Are you sure there's never been anything between you and that woman?" she asked teasingly. "Because Mali Kasam seems to be of more concern to you than she is to me. Mali does not bother me!"

Mason laughed with her. "I just want to make sure," he said, kissing her lips. "Mali can be quite a handful."

"If I need to I have no problems putting Miss Mali in her place."

Mason nodded, grinning broadly. "Claim your man, baby!"

She leaned to kiss his mouth as the driver pulled into the home's driveway. "I've done that already and I'll make sure she understands that."

He winked at her, still chuckling softly as the driver pulled the door open for them to get out.

Overlooking Phuket's dramatic east coast and the natural beauty of famous Phang Nga Bay, the Kasam family villa overlooked a stunning vista of beautiful limestone islands, tiny beaches and secret coves. The location was secluded yet conveniently close to town. In one direction Phaedra noted the premier Mission Hills Golf Course and two marinas. The home was a melding of contemporary architecture with key elements of traditional Thai designs. The multimillion-dollar property was stunning.

Daniel Kasam greeted them at the door. "Mason! Phaedra! Welcome," the man said as he welcomed them into his home.

Mason shook the man's hand. "Thank you for having us, Daniel!"

"It's good to see you again, Mr. Kasam," Phaedra said politely as he kissed the back of her hand. He wrapped an arm around Phaedra's waist, guiding her to the center of the open space.

As they settled themselves down in his living room, a server came with a tray of cocktails, extending them in Phaedra's direction first, and then Mason's.

"Please have a drink," Daniel said, offering them two glasses of rice wine. "We must toast!"

Mason nodded as he clinked his glass with Phaedra's.

"So, are you enjoying Thailand, Phaedra?" Daniel asked.

"I am, very much so," Phaedra answered. "Mason has been showing me a wonderful time."

"My friend is very good at that." He turned his attention back to Mason. "So, did you return for business, as well, my friend, or has this just been a pleasure trip?" The man winked an eye at Phaedra.

"Strictly pleasure," Mason said, his comment eliciting a giggle from Phaedra, who sat beside him.

Daniel nodded. "Finally! You are good for him, then, Phaedra. Mason has not had much success letting go of the business and just enjoying the pleasure."

Mason laughed. "Well, I'll be getting a lot of opportunity to practice. I sold my company recently."

"Well, well," Daniel replied, a look of surprise crossing his expression. "That is definitely something. This will be a significant change for you."

"I'm really hoping so, Daniel. You know that I've been ready for a change for some time, but enough about me. What is this I hear about you seeking the prime minister's seat?"

Daniel smiled, his head nodding. "You've heard right. It is definitely under consideration. With the political unrest becoming more problematic, especially with our young people, I have to consider all options which will be of benefit to my country."

For the next half hour Mason and Daniel chatted easily about their mutual business interests and thoughts on Daniel's political run and regaled Phaedra with stories about their many antics together. It was only as Daniel's personal chef called them for dinner that Mali arrived, sweeping into the room like a monsoon that would not be tamed. Rushing through the home's front door, she moved directly to Mason's side, throwing her arms around his neck to hug him tightly. Her father shook his head in annoyance.

"Mali!" he chastised, voicing his displeasure with his daughter's behavior.

The young woman rolled her eyes. Mason reached

for her arms, disentangling himself from her grasp. He gave her a light kiss against the back of her hand, then spun her toward the other side of the room. Mali huffed as she threw herself down against a cushioned chair, her arms crossed in defiance over her chest.

"You don't love me anymore, Mason!" she cried, pouting.

Mason shook his head. "I have much love for you, Mali."

"We all do, Mali. But you are quite the nuisance, daughter," Daniel added. "And you need to politely say hello to our guests."

"Yeah, hey," she said as she cut an eye in Phaedra's direction, crudely chewing on a piece of gum in her mouth. She refocused her attention back on Mason.

"It's a pleasure to see you again, Mali," Phaedra said as she casually dropped her hand against Mason's knee.

The gesture did not go unnoticed as Mali glared, rolled her eyes and then stormed off in the direction of the dining room. Daniel shook his head as he admonished the girl a second time, tossing his hands up in frustration.

Mason looked at Phaedra, who was smiling slyly, clearly amused. He shook his head. The two men locked eyes.

"Women!" Mason said to his friend, chuckling softly.

Daniel nodded in agreement. "I apologize for that one. It is my fault that she is as spoiled as she is. Her mother died when she was just a baby and I have always given her everything she has wanted." He gestured for them to follow him into the dining room, promising a sumptuous meal the likes of which guaranteed to exceed every one of their expectations.

As Phaedra followed, Mason on her heels, she couldn't help thinking that Mali's daddy clearly hadn't been able to get the girl everything because Mason Boudreaux was high on the woman's want list and unable to be had.

Aloud, she spoke to Mali, who'd already taken a seat at the table. "Mali, I hear you're a fashion student in London. That's every exciting," she said as she took the seat beside the other woman, the seat that Mali had been holding for Mason.

Mali eyed her with disdain, not at all pleased as Mason sat down in the seat across from the two women. Daniel made himself comfortable at the head of the table.

"I don't do that anymore," Mali said, turning her attention back to Phaedra. "It bored me."

"Oh, well, I'm sorry to hear that."

"Mali drops out of school every other week," her father interjected.

"I'm coming to the States for school," Mali said. "Phoenix, maybe." She tossed Mason a look and a smile.

Mason shook his head.

"Phoenix is beautiful," Phaedra said. "What do you think you'd like to study?"

Mali shrugged. "What do you do?" she asked, responding with a question of her own.

"I'm a photojournalist. Professional photography is my passion."

"So you take pictures," Mali said unenthusiastically.

"Award-winning pictures," Mason interjected. "Phaedra is considered one of the best in the world," he said proudly.

"Hmmph!" Mali grunted.

Phaedra laughed. "You're still young, Mali. One day you'll figure out what you want to do and I'm sure you'll be the best at it that you can be."

Not bothering to respond, Mali pulled a forkful of rice into her mouth, her attention dropping to the food on her plate. The rest of the evening was uneventful and before they were served dessert, Mali politely excused herself from the table.

"Where are you going?" Daniel asked. He swiped a cloth napkin across his mouth, then dropped it back into his lap.

His daughter strolled to the other side of the table and leaned to kiss Mason on his closed mouth. As she pulled back, she lifted her eyes to meet Phaedra's and Phaedra smiled in response, not even bothering to blink an eyelash.

Mali sighed. "I have some things to take care of," she said. "I'll see you again soon, Mason?"

Mason cleared his throat, then shook his head no. "Tomorrow is our last day here. Phaedra and I have to be back in Texas by the end of the week."

Mali tossed Phaedra another look as she made her way out the door. "Well, until I see you again, then," she said.

"It was nice meeting you, Mali," Phaedra called behind her.

As Daniel excused himself to follow behind his daughter, Phaedra pointed her index finger in Mason's direction. She leaned across the table as she whispered teasingly just loud enough for him to hear, "We'll need to disinfect your lips the minute we get home."

His eyes widening, Mason swiped the back of his fingers across his mouth, and both burst out laughing as the home's front door slammed harshly in the distance.

Chapter 13

The sun was setting in the distance as Mason and Phaedra sat on the beach, where the clear blue water kissed the white sand. Phaedra was nestled between Mason's legs, her back resting against his chest. A warm breeze wafted through the air as the sky above their heads shimmered in shades of red, orange and yellow. Neither could remember the last time they'd been so at ease, completely relaxed and content in the moment.

Phaedra blew a soft sigh as Mason drew his hands over her shoulders and down the lengths of her arms, his caress a slow and easy touch that teased each of her nerve endings.

"This is nice," she said softly, her voice a low whisper.

He pressed a gentle kiss against the back of her neck, allowing his lips to linger against the soft flesh.

His eyes were closed as he fell into the simplicity of the moment. It was nice. Nice in a way that couldn't be sufficiently explained. So nice that there was no one, and nothing, on either of their minds but each other. Mason blew a soft sigh against her skin, kissing her once again.

Nestling closer to him, Phaedra couldn't help wishing that life could always be this pleasant. She'd been wishing for moments like this since she was a little girl believing in fairy tales and the possibility of happily ever after. Her mother had always assured her that her crown prince would come when she least expected him, riding in like a knight in shining armor to save her from herself. Phaedra couldn't help thinking he'd finally found his way to her, his arms holding her tight to him, the wealth of the emotion he had for her undeniable. She had hardly been looking, and just like that, with the snap of her camera capturing his magnetic smile, Mason had steeled his way into her heart.

Mason gave her a hug, rolling her down against the blanket beneath them. He pressed his body over hers as he met her lips in a deep kiss. When he drew back, joy was shining in his eyes and in hers. He had no desire to move, wanting only to hover above her and admire the beauty before him.

As if she'd read his thoughts, her rich, full lips stretched into the happiest smile he had ever seen, highlighted by a light sheen of lip gloss that accentuated her warm, creamy complexion. Her nose wrinkled slightly as she smiled and her eyes gleamed with lust that was waiting to be coaxed out. Her body was silhouetted against the plush blanket beneath them, the curve of her hips and shapely legs and the natural form of her breasts stirring something animalistic within him. He could feel himself lengthening in his swim trunks, his body craving every last ounce of her sweetness.

Phaedra pulled a hand through her tousled hair, yet every hair seemed in place, framing her face nicely. Mason suddenly had visions of their future together, them sharing a rich and full life, traveling the world, making love in unimaginable places. He suddenly had an endless list of places where he wanted to have her, against a volcanic waterfall, in the midst of a garden of wildflowers in a mountain meadow, in the backseat of his Maybach parked on the French Riviera. As he pondered the possibilities he remained motionless, his breathing shallow, as if him breathing heavily might interrupt the beauty of the moment.

Heat spiraled between them, so abundant that Mason felt as if he could cut it with a knife. Phaedra felt it, too, and she began to pant softly, her lips parting as she passed the tip of her tongue between them. She purred softly, a low hum seeping past her open mouth. She lifted herself up just enough to pull his mouth back to hers, kissing him deeply a second time. When she pulled away, Mason was rock hard, the length of steel between his legs flexing for attention.

"What are you thinking?" Phaedra whispered as she nuzzled her face against his neck, wrapping her arms around his torso.

"I was just thinking that you are so beautiful and that sky is so spectacular that I should be making love to you."

Phaedra giggled. "I kind of like how you think!" she said as Mason nibbled the spot beneath her chin, teasing up to plant another kiss on her lips. He grabbed both her wrists as he lowered his weight against her, his body kissing her body. Phaedra opened her legs as he dropped himself between them, her torso captured beneath his. She began to slowly grind her pelvis against his, his erection straining hard against her.

As Mason stared down into her eyes, he could feel his control starting to slip away, so enamored with her he felt completely lost in her intense stare. He drew the fingers of his right hand down the length of her arm and Phaedra shivered, a flash of heat burning deep between her legs.

Mason slid his left arm beneath her body, pulling her tight against him as Phaedra snuggled her face into Mason's neck. She inhaled the sweetness of his warm brown skin, almost tasting the scent of his smooth chocolate body. Unable to resist, she planted a trail of gentle kisses against his neck and Mason groaned at the electric shivers that coursed through his body.

"Stop teasing me," Phaedra whispered, eager to experience the moment.

Mason softly stroked her hair, her dark tresses cascading against her shoulders. "I'm not teasing," he answered, a wry smile pulling at his mouth.

Mason took a finger and traced soft circles down the side of Phaedra's face. He twinked her nose and Phaedra giggled softly. When he reached her full lips, Phaedra grinned as he gently tapped the moist flesh. She opened her mouth and captured his firm digit between her lips. She sucked softly on the sweet flesh, using her cheek muscles to draw him in and out. When she sucked harder on his thick finger, Mason moaned, warm waves of excitement passing through him.

"Now *you're* teasing!" he said with a low chuckle.

Phaedra slipped his finger out of her mouth, kissed his warm palm, then rubbed her cheek against his hand. Mason leaned in and pressed his mouth to hers. He moaned and panted as Phaedra's tongue entered the heat of his mouth, their kiss deepening as she gripped the back of his head and locked her fingers against his tight curls. The kiss was passionate and promising, nourishing each other's intense desire. Their deep hunger for affection consumed them, causing them both to moan in ecstasy.

It seemed like an eternity before Mason broke the connection, both of them gasping excitedly for air. He pulled at the ribbon that held up her bathing suit top, then snatched the garment from around her body. He began kissing down her body, running his hands down the length of her torso as he nuzzled his nose between her breasts. She had beautiful breasts, Mason thought, like fresh-picked vine-ripened peaches. He ran his hands back up her sides and kissed the inner curve of her left peach.

He looked up at her. Phaedra had her eyes closed and was breathing harder than she was before. He took one of her nipples into his mouth and started sucking and swirling his tongue around the sweet delight while he gently caressed and kneaded the other breast. Phaedra groaned with pleasure beneath his ministrations, the heat from his fingertips lingering against her skin. When he switched sides and began suckling on her other breast, Phaedra was completely gone.

With mastered skill Mason continued to slide down the length of her body, his moist kisses stopping at her belly button as he dipped his tongue into the slight well. At the waistband of her bikini bottoms, he paused and

Phaedra groaned at the loss of contact. She opened her eyes to watch as he hooked his fingers into her bottoms and pulled them down, his fingers connecting with precision against her flesh. She lifted her hips as he pulled them off, throwing them somewhere into the sand.

He paused as he looked at her. "God, you are so beautiful!" he said, his tone intoxicating.

Before she could respond he began to minister to the bundle of swollen flesh that pulsed between her legs, his fingers tapping with magic. Phaedra fell into a trance of pleasure. "Oh, Mason..." She bit down against her bottom lip, knowing that she wouldn't last long if he continued to stroke her so unabashedly.

Phaedra inhaled swiftly, the magnitude of him and the moment suddenly consuming. Never before had anything felt more perfect to her. She sat up, reaching to pull him back to her. She tugged at his shorts, running her hands across his stomach as she pulled the string to loosen his swim trunks while he kissed her. Mason stopped kissing her long enough to stand up, slide his trunks down and step out of them. Pulling out a condom hidden in his pocket, he sheathed himself quickly.

Grabbing his hands Phaedra guided him back down to her. She closed her eyes and moaned at the skin to skin contact as he rolled against her. She started to grind her hips with his, the two moving in perfect sync. Phaedra kissed his neck as he ran his hands through her hair. With perfect precision he entered her easily, the two dancing together as if they were one body and not two. She pushed as he pushed, pulled as he pulled, meeting him stroke for stroke.

Mason panted, his excitement building as sheer decadence surged through every nerve and muscle in his body. Phaedra lost all coherent thought, her body convulsing with waves of pure, unadulterated pleasure. She arched her back against him, calling his name into the night air.

"Mason! Oh, Mason," she screamed, her body juddering around his as Mason spilled himself deep inside her.

As they climaxed simultaneously, Mason clung to her, feeling as if he'd never be able to get enough of the exquisite creature. When he collapsed on top of her, Phaedra clutched him tightly to her. Her chest moved up and down against his as they both fought to catch their breaths. With stars spiraling above her head, love spilled from Phaedra's eyes as she met his stare, unable to miss the longing that shimmered in the dark orbs. Above them, sitting high in the darkened sky, a full moon gave them its blessing.

Mason and Phaedra spent hours on the beach, the night air beginning to cool comfortably. With one last dip in the warm waters of the lagoon, they strolled hand in hand back to his bungalow. Phaedra lay on her stomach, sprawled across his king-size bed as Mason nuzzled his body against hers, both unable to sleep.

"This feels too good to be true," Phaedra whispered.

Mason nodded his understanding, his hand stroking her lower back and the curve of her buttocks. "But it's all very real," he whispered back.

Phaedra smiled sweetly, shifting so that she could kiss the curve of his shoulder. "But all good things must come to an end," she concluded, a deep sigh easing out of her mouth.

"It doesn't have to," Mason said. "This can last as long as you want it to."

"What if I want forever?"

Mason laughed, a low chuckle that warmed Phaedra's spirit. "Then you can have forever."

"You have such a way with words, Mr. Boudreaux." She smiled.

"I am quite the wordsmith, madame, and your wishes are my commands."

"You could spoil a girl like that."

"Have no doubts, I plan to spoil my girl like that."

Phaedra eased herself farther into his side, heat wafting from his skin to hers. "I like how that sounds. I like being your girl."

Mason leaned over to kiss her forehead, brushing his lips gently against her. "That makes me very happy," he whispered against her skin, the warmth of his breath causing her to shiver ever so slightly.

"I want to make you very happy," Phaedra said coyly. She stroked his chest, gently grazing the broad expanse of flesh with her fingernails. Mason inhaled sharply at the sensation, blood surging in a southern direction. "Don't move," she commanded when he tried to reach for her.

His body tensed with anticipation as she pushed him back against the mattress. She drew her hand down past his belly button, pausing at the cusp of his pubic hair. Her fingers teased the tight black curls and his erection twitched eagerly, the protrusion stretching obscenely.

When he couldn't wait any longer Mason took her hand and wrapped it around the length of his manhood. Her hand quivered as her fingers touched the long, thick, rock-hard length. Phaedra began to stroke him gently, feeling the long shaft as her palm glided up and down.

Mason shuddered as her fingers danced over his flesh and he sighed audibly. Phaedra was in awe as she stared at him, his beautiful, big organ seeming to grow beneath her nurturing. He was so hard and hot, silky to her touch, and as she moved her hand gently back and forth she could feel his heartbeat pulsing rhythmically in the palm of her hand. The tips of her fingers glided against his testicles and Mason jumped from the sensation. The feelings were exquisite and he could feel himself weakening beneath her touch.

As she continued to stroke him, her motions becoming more intense, he lifted his hips to grind against her palm. His hands clutched the sheet beneath him as he allowed his body to give in to the intensity. His breathing began to quicken and Mason knew that he couldn't hold on as Phaedra took him over the edge. He suddenly shuddered, his body shaking all over. His orgasm flooded over her hand and arm as the woman continued to milk him dry.

As the last remnants of his climax lulled him to a comfortable slumber, Phaedra nuzzled her mouth against his ear and whispered, "Sweet dreams."

Chapter 14

Phaedra woke well before Mason, the man snoring comfortably at her side. Rising from the bed, she tiptoed into the bathroom. Staring at her reflection in the mirror, she couldn't believe that she was as wide-awake as she was. It had only been a few short hours since she and Mason had fallen asleep together. Any other time or place and she'd be a walking zombie, desperate for one more hour of slumber.

After splashing cold water on her face and brushing her teeth to a pearl-white sheen, she tiptoed back into the bedroom. Her clothes were in the other bungalow so she borrowed one of Mason's T-shirts, slipping the oversize top around her naked body. Sliding into a pair of rubber flip-flops, she grabbed her camera from the dresser and eased her way outside, mindful not to disturb Mason's rest.

Outside, the sun was rising, the beginning rays of

light just starting to crease the dark sky. Phaedra was glad for the moment, wanting to capture the morning's sunrise. They were headed back to Bangkok today, then back to the United States tomorrow, and despite the many hours they'd spent alone on the island, there was much Phaedra had yet to experience of the private landscape.

As she walked the length of beach, photographing the early morning imagery, she was taken aback by the sheer beauty of the lush landscape. The tropical topography was like nothing Phaedra had ever experienced before and she knew Thailand would forever be one of her favorite places in the world. She adjusted the fifty-millimeter prime lens on her camera to accommodate the low light conditions and capture the more minute details of the flora.

Maneuvering her way past the length of beach, she eased her way into the natural forest, snapping shot after shot of the diverse plant life. Before long she'd gathered a nice visual collection of the bamboo, coconut palms and banana trees posed against the morning sky.

Not wanting Mason to worry if he woke and couldn't find her, she eased her way back to the beach, a fresh-picked bunch of bananas in her hand. As she strolled casually across the sandy stretch she thought back to the evening before when Mason had made love to her right where she now stood. A bright smile flooded her expression and a shiver of heat coursed in the pit of her stomach. The man gave her butterflies and just the sheer thought of him sent her into sensory overload.

She paused, inhaling the scent of the ocean, the warm morning air a soothing balm to her spirit. In the distance she could hear a boat approaching, the deep roar of the engine out of place in the midst of all the quiet. Mason must have heard it, as well, because just as she peered across the lagoon in the direction of the approaching vessel, he stepped outside.

She waved excitedly at the sight of him, but Mason was focused on the speedboat, not looking in her direction. After resting the bananas on the sand at her feet, she switched out the lens for the two-hundred-millimeter telephoto lens and lifted her camera to her eyes. After making the necessary adjustments, she zoomed in on his face. His expression was pensive, an air of uncertainty seeming to drop down against the man's broad shoulders. She snapped the shot, noting the concern in his dark eyes.

Phaedra lowered her camera briefly, still staring, something about his demeanor giving her pause, her heart beginning to race. Mason hadn't said anything about expecting visitors, she thought, wondering if the boat's occupants were an unexpected intrusion. She was almost certain that it wasn't the island's elderly caretakers, Bahn and his wife, Rutana. They came every day by canoe, their arrival almost covert as the narrow boat cut through the water with an easy, quiet precision.

As the speedboat came to a quick stop at the end of the dock, Mason strolled casually in its direction. Phaedra lifted her camera a second time as two men hopped out of the boat, appearing to greet him. She snapped one photo and then a second and she was poised to take a third when there was a sudden rush of loud chatter, the trio appearing to argue. Phaedra looked over the top of her camera, her anxiety rising tenfold. She peered back through the lens just as the taller of the two strangers struck Mason with something in his hand. Phaedra gasped loudly, her heart skipping a quick beat, then two. As Mason fell to his knees the other man threw a canvas sack over Mason's head and, like that, they tossed his body into the boat, jumped in behind him and gunned the boat's engine.

Still snapping shot after shot, Phaedra struggled to keep her camera focused on what was happening. Then without thinking she began to run, desperation taking hold as she screamed out his name. By the time she made it to the other side of the beach and the end of the dock, the speedboat had rounded the north corner of the island, Mason disappearing from her sight.

Phaedra was at wit's end. She'd been in the custody of the Thai Royal Police for over three hours trying to get someone to understand that Mason Boudreaux was in trouble. But nothing she said could convince them of the urgency. She pulled her hands frantically through her hair, pacing the small interrogation room she'd been left in. The officer who'd taken her statement had been exceptionally cooperative when she'd mentioned Mason's name, but even that hadn't been enough to motivate him to start searching.

Dropping down onto a metal chair, Phaedra closed her eyes and tears began to fall rapidly. For whatever reasons, after Mason had been taken, she hadn't been able to get any reception on her cell phone. Waiting for Bahn and Rutana to arrive had felt like forever. Bahn had saved the moment, though, ushering her to the mainland and the police department, promising that he and Rutana would pack her and Mason's belongings and get her to wherever she needed to go when she needed to move. Now she was anxious to go do anything that would help find Mason. She jumped to her feet, the chair crashing from beneath her, the sound ringing like thunder against the concrete floor. Shaking, Phaedra clenched her fists at her sides, fighting not to scream out loud.

Just as she was about to throw a major tantrum, the door swung open, Officer Don Niran eyeing her curiously. "Is everything okay, miss?" he asked politely.

"No!" Phaedra screamed, desperately trying to contain her emotions. "Nothing is okay. Mason Boudreaux is missing and no one is doing anything to help me find him."

The officer nodded, his expression blank. "I assure you, miss, we are doing everything we can to corroborate your story. However, it is more plausible that Mr. Boudreaux simply left without telling you where he was going. As you said, you've just recently become acquainted with him. Perhaps you didn't know the man as well as you thought?"

Phaedra bristled, her eyes narrowing sharply. She took a deep breath. "Well," she said, "I can appreciate your opinion, Officer Niran, but I assure you, I know him very well and I know what I saw."

"That being so, miss, these things take time. So, if there is nothing else that you can tell us, I must get back to my duties."

It was on the tip of Phaedra's tongue to argue, but knowing that such would probably not be in her best interest she simply nodded. Clearly, she needed help, and help wasn't going to be found here.

The officer turned to the door, moving as if to make an exit, before Phaedra called after him.

"Yes, miss?"

"Please, is it possible for me to use a telephone to place an international telephone call? I need to call my family to let them know what has happened and to make arrangements to get back home," she said, meeting his gaze evenly.

Officer Niran paused briefly before nodding. "Certainly, miss," he responded after a quick second. "Whatever I can do to be of assistance to you."

Chapter 15

John's cell phone ringing pulled him out of a deep sleep. For a brief moment he thought he might be dreaming, but the ring tone persisted, disturbing the quiet in his bedroom. Beside him, Marah muttered incoherently, rolling onto her side as she wrapped herself around a pillow and pulled the sheet above her head.

Leaning toward the nightstand, John grabbed his phone, squinting to see the caller ID. The display read UNKNOWN. For a brief second he thought about ignoring it, but something in the pit of his stomach wouldn't let him. Flipping the device open, he pulled it awkwardly to his ear.

"Hello?" he said, the lazy drone of sleep punctuating his tone.

On the other end Phaedra's voice pierced the airwaves. She sounded as if she was on the verge of hysteria. "John, I'm sorry to wake you but something has happened to Mason and I can't get anyone to help me find him and I don't know what to do. I'm scared and please, I need someone to help me and I didn't know who else to call," she said, barely pausing to take a breath as the words rushed out of her mouth.

"Calm down," John said as he sat up in the bed. Tossing a quick glance toward Marah's sleeping form, he whispered into the receiver, "Tell me what's happened."

Phaedra nodded as if he could see her. Taking a deep breath, she told him what had happened from the moment Mason had stepped out onto the dock to when the Thai police had allowed her to use their office telephone to make a call. She repeated verbatim every conversation she'd had since waking, and with every other sentence she kept reiterating how scared she was. By the end of telling her story she fought back tears thinking of the worst possible outcome.

Wide-awake, John tried to be as consoling as the distance between them would allow. "Phaedra, I need you to relax, okay? I'm on my way and if Mason hasn't shown up by the time I get there, I promise I will do whatever it takes to find him."

Phaedra's head bobbed up and down against her thin neck. "Thank you," she whispered, the words catching in her throat. "Thank you so much!"

"How are you traveling?" John asked. "Do you have transportation?"

"Yes. Mason's housekeeper is being really helpful."

"Good. I want you to go to the Boudreaux Residence Resort and ask for the general manager. His name is Sean Martine. As soon as I hang up with you I'm going to call him. He'll take care of you until I can get there."

"Sean Martine," she repeated. "Okay."

"And, Phaedra, I do not want you running around Phuket trying to find Mason by yourself. I don't want anything to happen to you. Do you understand me?"

Another tear rolled over her cheek. "Yes," she finally answered, swiping at her eyes with the back of her hand. "John? He's going to be okay, isn't he?"

John took a deep breath as he swung his legs off the side of the bed. "Don't you worry. Everything is going to be fine," he said. "I'll see you soon."

As he disconnected the call, John released a deep sigh. He'd promised Phaedra that things were going to be okay, but truth be told he wasn't so sure. If Mason was in trouble, their being out of the country was going to make finding him difficult at best. As he shook Marah awake, he pressed the speed-dial button on his cell phone. He needed to round up the troops. He wasn't sure himself where to begin, but he imagined this was a mission that was going to take more than himself to accomplish successfully.

Three hours later the Stallion jet was fueled and ready on the tarmac, the pilot waiting for John to order their takeoff. Both John and Matthew were on their cell phones, still issuing commands and asking questions. Half a day would pass before they reached Thailand, and knowing how things could change in that amount of time, no one wanted to take any unnecessary chances.

Once John was assured that Phaedra was safely secreted away in the owner's suite of the hotel, he was better able to fathom what had actually happened and how they might discover Mason's whereabouts.

Matthew put one call on hold to answer another. John smiled ever so slightly as he heard his brother trying to calm his wife's nerves. "Katrina, you need to stop worrying, baby....I'll do my best....I promise, honey....Katrina, you just need to concentrate on taking care of yourself and our baby....I will...I will...I will make sure your brother is okay....Yes, dear! Yes... I'll call you as soon as we get there and find out what's going on," he finally concluded before disconnecting the call.

The two brothers locked gazes. Matthew shook his head. "This isn't good, is it?"

John took a deep breath. "I've spoken to the Thai police, who are less than helpful, to Mason's housekeeper, who knows nothing, and the hotel staff, who were close to him, and no one has any idea what's going on," he said firmly.

"When you speak with Marah, please make her promise to stay by my wife's side. I don't need her going into labor before I can get back here."

John nodded. "I've already handled it for you, brother. Marah will make sure Katrina takes care of herself."

"So will Mitch," Mark said as he stepped onto the plane, entering the conversation.

"Hey," John said, rising. He and Mark bumped shoulders in greeting. Matthew tipped his head, the two men slapping palms.

"What do we know so far?" Mark questioned as he took a seat in one of the leather chairs.

John gestured toward the pilot, nodding his consent. "Let's get in the air first and I'll fill you in," he said.

An hour or so later the three brothers had settled

down for the long flight, dozing comfortably in their seats. With the thirteen-hour time difference it would be late when they arrived in Thailand, and what they might be able to accomplish at that hour of the night would be slim. But each of them knew they needed to be as rested as possible if the next few days proved to be the challenge they predicted they would be.

Phaedra was stir-crazy as she stood at the front desk of the luxury hotel waiting for the general manager. Since her arrival the staff had been exceptionally gracious, extending her every courtesy. But she couldn't sit in the luxury suite one minute longer and not do something. She strummed her fingernails against the marble counter as she waited, her patience having worn thin.

Sean Martine greeted her warmly, the tall blond man with the strong Nordic features moving to her side. "Miss Parrish, I apologize for keeping you waiting. I hope everything has met with your satisfaction."

Phaedra nodded. "Yes, definitely. I have no complaints and I can't tell you how much I appreciate everything you and your staff have done for me."

Mr. Martine smiled. "So, what else might I be able to do for you?"

"I was hoping that I could get access to a computer and a printer. Preferably a color printer?"

Mr. Martine paused in a moment of quick reflection. "I think that's possible. We have a color printer in the marketing department and plenty of computers. Why don't you follow me?" he said as he gestured toward the office doors.

Behind the scenes of the hotel, the back office was

a bustling whirlwind of employees ensuring that the mechanics of the Boudreaux Residence Resort worked smoothly, no guests having a clue that their perfect vacations might have come with some major bumps along the way.

In the marketing area Phaedra was directed to a small cubicle and given access to a computer and printer. Mr. Martine smiled and nodded politely as he instructed the employees to give her any assistance she might need. After expressing her sincerest appreciation and watching until he was out of the room and no one was looking over her shoulder, Phaedra finally relaxed the hold she'd had on her camera case, the instrument secured over her shoulder and beneath her arm.

She took a deep breath as she pulled the sixteen-gigabyte SanDisk CF memory card out of the camera, inserted it in the computer's SD slot and accessed the digital images she'd taken earlier that day. She had briefly thought of telling Officer Niran about the photographs, but something about his attitude and demeanor had stopped her. Instinctively, Phaedra had been certain that if she'd told and he'd confiscated her camera and pictures, they would never again have seen the light of day.

One by one Phaedra printed each image that she'd taken, enlarging them as much as the system would allow. An hour later she had a stack of sixty-plus photos and duplicate copies that had captured Mason's kidnapping. Sixty-plus images that put faces on the two men who'd taken him and the boat the three had ridden away in. After emailing the files to herself and stuffing the images into a manila folder, Phaedra headed back to her room to lay her head on a pillow and cry.

* * *

Mason woke to the stench of dead fish and a raging headache that made him feel as if his head were about to combust from the pressure. He took a deep breath, wincing from the pain and the sour smell that filled the air. The room was small, sparsely decorated, a concrete shelter with a single door and one window. He lay on the only piece of furniture in the room, a wire-framed bed with a paper-thin mattress that had seen better days. There was also a small plastic bucket in the corner and a week-old newspaper on the floor.

Struggling to his feet, Mason braced his hand against the stone wall to hold himself upright. The floor was cold and damp beneath his bare feet, grime and sludge the floor covering of choice. He was still wearing the sweatpants he'd slipped into when he'd heard the speedboat earlier. He was bare-chested and grateful for it since the temperature in the room was sweltering. A glass of ice water and a cold shower would have been a welcome comfort if he had a choice. He felt as if he'd been run over by a Mack truck, the throbbing across his temples making him nauseated. He gently pressed his fingers along his forehead, his hand coming away with streaks of drying blood. He tried to take another deep breath, wishing for just one breeze of fresh air.

As he expected, the door was locked and there was no doorknob on his side. Moving slowly to the window, he stepped up on his tiptoes to peer outside. He was somewhere on the eastern seaboard, the sun setting in the distance behind the building. Wherever he was, he was right on the coastline of one of the fishing villages, the salt air spraying the scent of the day's catch.

He didn't bother to call out, knowing that if there was anyone outside, they were not there to do him any good.

Moving back to the bed, Mason eased his body down. He couldn't begin to fathom why he was there or who was responsible. The two men from earlier had spoken to him in Siamese, the gun that was pointed at him announcing their intent. And then he'd been slapped with the butt of the weapon, the strike rendering him helpless. In that moment there had been only one thing on Mason's mind and it was still haunting him. Where was Phaedra and was she safe?

Chapter 16

Phaedra was pacing the room when the Stallion brothers finally arrived, knocking at the entrance for her attention. Pulling the door open, she could only have been happier if it had been Mason himself.

"Thank you!" Phaedra cried, throwing her arms around John's neck first and then Mark's. "Thank you so much," she said as she hugged Matthew in greeting.

"Have you heard anything at all from Mason?" John questioned, moving into the suite as he looked around.

"Nothing. I called the police station a few hours ago and they weren't able to tell me anything more than it was still being looked into."

"I don't think they're going to be of any use to us," Matthew said.

"And you can't tell us anything else?" Mark asked, his eyes meeting Phaedra's.

"I can do better than that," she said, reaching for

the manila folder on the glass coffee table. "I can show you." She passed the folder to Mark, cutting her eyes from him to John and Matthew, then back. "I was on the far end of the beach when the boat pulled up to the dock. I was taking pictures of the landscape. I kept taking pictures."

Mark was flipping through the images, his brothers peering over his shoulder. "These are good," he said, turning to look at Phaedra. "Really good. They should help."

Before Phaedra could respond the telephone rang, startling them all. She moved to the other side of the room to the oak desk to answer it.

"Hello?"

"Yes, miss. This is Lina at the front desk. I'm trying to reach Mr. John Stallion, please," a woman with a soft voice said on the other end.

"One moment," Phaedra answered, gesturing toward John. "It's for you, John," she said, eyeing him curiously.

John moved to her side and took the receiver from her hand. "This is John Stallion," he said as the others stood waiting.

Phaedra chewed nervously on her bottom lip, her heart beginning to race. Sensing her rising stress, Matthew moved beside her, wrapping a warm arm around her shoulders. The gesture caught Phaedra off guard, but she was grateful for the compassion. She blew a soft sigh.

"Send them up," John said just before he set the receiver back onto the hook. "We have company," he said, looking from one curious face to the other. "The cavalry has arrived."

Matthew nodded, a wide smile pulling at his lips. "Just in time," he said softly as he gently hugged Phaedra to him.

Almost as quickly as Matthew had spoken, there was a knock on the door, a heavy *rap, rap, rap* looking for attention. He moved to the door and opened it, greeting their visitors warmly. "Please, come in," John said. "It's good to see you again. I just wish it was under different circumstances."

Three men and a woman stepped through the door and for a brief second Phaedra was certain that Mason Boudreaux had been cloned at least once if not four times over.

John made the introductions. "Phaedra, allow me to introduce you to Mason's sister Kamaya and his brothers, Donovan, Guy and Kamaya's twin, Kendrick."

The woman smiled warmly. "Hi, it's nice to meet you. We've heard a lot about you," she said, reaching to give Phaedra a warm hug.

"It's nice to meet you, too," Phaedra responded.

The brothers all echoed their sister's sentiments as they moved around the room shaking hands and reacquainting themselves with the family they'd first met at their sister Katrina's wedding to Matthew.

Guy Boudreaux was most anxious to get down to business. "So, where are we?" he said as they all settled down in the living room space. "What's the game plan?"

Mark pulled one of the images from the folder. "We need to track down these two," he said, passing the photo to Guy, who passed it on to his siblings. "And that means we need to hit the streets."

"Do we even know why someone would do this?"

Phaedra ventured to question, feeling as if she was missing something.

Donovan Boudreaux leaned forward in his seat. Of the brothers he looked most like Mason, the resemblance almost eerie. "Phaedra, Mason has a lot of history here in Thailand. Building this hotel required him to deal with a lot of people, some who might have been a little unsavory. And as I'm sure you already know, the political climate has some challenges. Although he made some great friends, there were just as many who didn't want him or the hotel here and who haven't been overly accommodating."

Guy nodded. "He owes a lot of his success here to Daniel Kasam. Daniel helped him navigate the political waters. The man pulled some strings that many thought were impossible."

"I met Daniel. And his daughter. We all had dinner the other night," Phaedra noted.

"He's a great guy but he's rumored to have some ties with the Bangkok crime syndicate," Guy said, adding the disclaimer, "not that we're sure that's true. He might not be a Mafia lord."

He continued. "I do know, though, that there were some who were not happy about the connection between them or that Mason was able to do what he did because of Daniel's help."

Phaedra stood up in frustration. "This is crazy. A crime syndicate? A Mafia lord? Really?"

Both Donovan and Guy shrugged.

"It is crazy," Kendrick interjected, "but they do things differently here. Traditionally, high officials were given gifts for rendering their services. In addition, they benefited from getting a percentage of their expenditures even if they didn't do anything. Obviously, the bigger the gifts they received, the bigger the payoff for the giver. The practice bred corruption. Unfortunately, Thailand has had a long history of dishonesty, from extortion and bribery to the use of insider information to even buy land. For many reasons, although it's not talked about, those practices are still deeply embedded in Thai society."

"So, do we need to speak with Daniel?" Phaedra asked. "To see what he might know?"

"Our first stop in the morning," John said. "Phaedra, you, Kamaya and I will pay Daniel a visit right after breakfast tomorrow. I've already called to schedule an appointment with him."

"Tonight, though," Mark interjected, "we need to hit the streets." He gestured with the picture in his hand. "Unsavory characters tend to keep their heads down during the day."

Kendrick stood up, reaching for the briefcase he'd arrived with. When he popped the lid, Phaedra was stunned by the amount of cash inside.

"We knew we were going to have to grease some palms to get some answers," he said, answering the question Phaedra was thinking but didn't want to ask. "We were able to exchange it for Thai baht at the airport."

Kendrick tossed two wrapped stacks of currency toward Mark and two toward his brother Guy, the men depositing the money in the breast pockets of their suit jackets. "Are you coming with us?" Kendrick asked, looking toward Donovan.

The man shook his head. "No. I need to follow up on some leads here in the hotel."

"I'll give you a hand with that," Matthew said.

"I'd appreciate that, brother-in-law," Donovan said as Kendrick closed the case and handed it to John.

John crossed over to the other side of the room. Sliding back a painting on the wall, he revealed a large wall safe. He pushed a series of codes on the digital panel, then depressed his thumb against the security guard. When the door swung open he deposited the case inside, closed the door, secured it and slid the painting back in place. "Everybody good?" he asked, turning to the other men in the room.

They all nodded.

"We ready to bounce?" Mark asked as he moved toward the door.

Kendrick and Guy were close on his heels.

"Stay safe," John admonished, pointing his index finger in their direction.

Kamaya then repeated John's wishes but with a hint of worry in her voice.

Guy leaned to kiss his sister's cheek. "We got this."

Donovan gestured for Matthew to follow him. "We need to move, as well," he said, winking at Phaedra.

Matthew and John slapped palms as the two men exited the room. When the door was closed behind them, John blew a deep sigh, tossing his head back against his shoulders. It had been an exceptionally long day and it was about to get even longer.

Phaedra was still wide-eyed awake, believing that she would never be able to sleep until they found Mason alive and well. On the other side of the king-size bed, his sister Kamaya was snoozing easily, seemingly without a care in the world. But Phaedra knew she was worried, too. They were all worried.

Much like with the Stallion family, there was no escaping the Boudreaux lineage. Their distinctive features hinted of an African-Asian ancestry, with their slight angular eyes, thin noses, high cheek lines and full, pouty lips. Donovan could easily have passed for Mason's twin, the low lines of their closely cropped haircuts complementing their facial features. Kendrick had the same facial features but had a full afro, boasting a retro, bad-boy facade. Guy was more bohemian in his look, rocking dreads that hung well past his broad shoulders. He had an artistic aura about him and even if she hadn't already known that he was in the entertainment industry, Phaedra would have easily taken him for a musician or an artist.

Like her sister Katrina's, Kamaya's features were soft, more delicate than their brothers'. But where Katrina's demeanor was exceptionally conservative, Kamaya was hard-core and edgy. And unlike the Stallion men who all boasted the same rich, dark, coffee-with-no-cream complexion, the Boudreauxes were a kaleidoscope of colorations that ranged from burned umber to milk chocolate.

Although she would have preferred to meet Mason's family under very different circumstances, it was what it was. Kamaya had emphasized that they'd heard a lot about her, and Phaedra couldn't help wondering what and from whom. Had Mason been there she knew it would have been a delightful laugh between them. She then curled her body into the fetal position as she clung to her side of the bed.

In the other room John was sleeping comfortably

on the couch, snoring easily. Phaedra was grateful for him, and for Mark and Matthew, the trio coming when she called without blinking an eye. Mark was still cautious, dealing with her at arm's length, but there was nothing hostile in his demeanor like before. She hadn't asked about the test results and no one had volunteered the conclusions. The question of her paternity and the familial connection between them still lingered in the back of her mind, but in that moment Phaedra wasn't interested in hearing the answers until Mason were there with her as he had been since she first came to Texas.

Chapter 17

Daniel Kasam rushed to greet them, almost pulling John and the two women through the front door of his home. Concern painted his expression, the man seemingly distressed to learn Mason was missing.

"This is very serious!" Daniel bellowed as he gestured for them to take a seat. "Very serious!"

"Obviously, you understand our concerns," John said.

"More than you know," Daniel said. He reached for an envelope resting on the table and passed it to John. "This was delivered to my office right after I spoke with you yesterday."

Taking the mailer from the man, John lifted a typed letter from inside and read its contents. He looked up to meet Daniel's gaze, then dropped his eyes back to the letter to read one more time. He took a deep breath as he passed the document to Phaedra and Kamaya to read.

"A million dollars!" Phaedra yelled. "They want a million dollars in ransom?"

"I'm afraid so, Phaedra. Unscrupulous, it is," the man said as he rose to his feet and paced the floor.

"Why did they send it to you?" Phaedra queried. "Does this have anything to do with Mason's business dealings?"

Daniel shook his head. "There are some people Mason had to do business with who were not good people. I'm sure with him selling his business one of them thought this would be a good opportunity to take advantage. However, I assure you it has nothing to do with any transactions Mason and I had between us."

John cut his eye at Phaedra, his stare moving her to reflect on the other man's tone. Daniel seemed insulted by her suggestion and Phaedra was cautious not to offend him further.

"Well, we should take this to the police," she said.

Daniel nodded. "I have already given a copy to Officer Niran. I was made to understand that he is handling this case? Is that correct?"

John nodded. "That's correct. I'll touch base with him as soon as we leave."

"You should do that," Daniel said. "The sooner you pay the ransom, I'm sure the sooner they will let Mason go."

Phaedra took a deep breath. "Do you think Mali might be able to give us any information about Mason's acquaintances? Is she here by chance?"

Daniel turned his back to the conversation, reaching to pass each of them a glass of fresh-squeezed mango-and-papaya juice. "I'm sure Mali knows nothing. And unfortunately, she has already left Thailand.

She's gone back to school," he said as he gave Phaedra a slight smile.

Phaedra's face skewed with confusion. She opened her mouth to speak, then closed it, shooting John a quick glance as she bit back her words.

John smiled politely. "Well, we certainly appreciate your time, Mr. Kasam. You've been a big help to us."

"Of course," Daniel said. "If I can do anything else to assist you, please just ask. Everything I have is at your disposal."

"We greatly appreciate that," Kamaya added.

"Where did you say Mali was going to school?" Phaedra asked as Daniel clasped her hand beneath his.

"Design school in London," he answered matter-of-factly. He kissed the backs of Phaedra's fingers. "I'm sure Mason will show up before you know it," he said, adding, "As soon as you pay their demands. I'll call you as soon as they contact me with the details of the exchange."

Phaedra lifted her mouth in a slight smile, her expression not as certain. "Thank you," she said, biting back what she wanted to say. "You've been a good friend," she added for conversation's sake, not believing one word.

Daniel waved his goodbyes as their driver pulled the car out of his driveway. As they headed in the direction of the hotel, Phaedra met John's curious stare.

"What is it, Phaedra?" he asked.

She shook her head. "What are we going to do? They want one million dollars!"

John nodded. His tone was consoling. "The money isn't the problem," he said. "We have the money. What we need to figure out is if we should pay it. The fact remains that we might pay and they might not let Mason go. We need to keep trying to figure out who did this and where they might be holding him."

She blew a deep breath, trusting that John knew best. She thought about their meeting with Daniel, everything about their conversation bothering her, and she said so. "Daniel never said why he thought they sent the ransom note directly to him. And he also lied. Daniel lied to us."

"What do you mean?" Kamaya asked, leaning forward in her seat.

"Mali didn't go back to school. At dinner the other night Mali told us she quit school. She had no plans to go back."

"Interesting," John pondered. "And something else. I spoke with Niran this morning. He didn't say anything about the ransom note or that he'd spoken with Daniel."

"I don't like that man," Phaedra said, "and there's nothing about him or Daniel that I trust."

"But why do you think Daniel would lie about his daughter?" John questioned.

Kamaya answered before Phaedra had a chance to. "Mali Kasam is obsessed with Mason. That girl has been like fungus since the first day Mason stepped foot in Thailand, and her father indulges her every whim."

Phaedra nodded. "What Mali wants…" she said, not bothering to finish the statement as she turned to stare out the window.

Mason had fallen asleep, the pain in his skull still throbbing with a vengeance. It was dark when he woke and he had no sense of the time. He could have been sleeping for hours, or days; he just wasn't sure.

He sat up slowly, his equilibrium clearly off-kilter. While he slept someone had paid him a visit. A cardboard box had been dropped in the center of the floor. A tray of food—two sandwiches wrapped in waxed paper, three pieces of fruit, a bag of Thai cookies and a gallon jug of water left for him to consume.

An old oil lantern was burning on low, emitting just enough light for him to see how to maneuver his way around. Mason sighed. He was still in the dark about what his kidnappers wanted. But clearly they didn't want him dead. Not yet. He thought about the people he knew and he drew a blank as he reasoned who might want to do this to him.

He'd always been as aboveboard in his business dealings as was possible in Thailand, determined to maintain his integrity. And even in those situations where he might have consorted with individuals whose tactics were questionable, he had kept those dealings on the up-and-up. So he was drawing a blank, and the pain in his head wasn't helping him.

He took a deep breath and then a second. The temperature had started to cool, a breeze of fresh air billowing through the concrete opening. It was quiet outside, the hiss of ocean water the only sound. Mason's frustration was rapidly rising. If nothing else he needed to know that Phaedra was safe from harm. It had been clear in the moments before everything went completely blank that the two intruders were only interested in him.

But where had she disappeared to? Waking to an empty bed shouldn't have been different, but without Phaedra by his side, his whole world felt as if it had changed. It had taken no time at all for him to find comfort in her presence, thankful to have her next to him when he fell asleep, grateful to wake up by her side. But Phaedra hadn't been in his bed that morning. Phaedra had been gone and Mason had missed her desperately. Wanting to find Phaedra had been the last thing on his mind before their peace and quiet had been stormed.

Mason closed his eyes as he lay back down. He need to rest, to soothe the hurt that beat like thunder behind his eyes. He anticipated needing his strength to free himself from captivity, and if any harm had come to Phaedra, he would need every ounce of his might to cause a world of hurt to whoever was responsible.

After John had called the rest of the family to share news of the ransom note, they all converged back at the hotel suite. When they arrived Mark's excitement was hard for him to contain.

"I think we found them," Mark said, tossing a Polaroid onto the table. "They were at Club Pattaya until four o'clock this morning."

"Where did they go from there?" John asked.

Guy answered. "An apartment in downtown Phuket. Above the fruit market."

"We need to go back. We need to talk to them," Phaedra said as she took the photo from John's hand. "We need to find out what they know."

Her eyes suddenly widened as she studied the picture Mark had taken, playing as if he were just a tourist enjoying the Thai nightlife. She tapped a manicured finger against the image, her own excitement suddenly infectious. "This woman here in the background, was she with them?" Phaedra asked, looking from Mark to Guy and then Donovan.

Mark shrugged as he leaned to stare where Phaedra was pointing. "They spoke like they knew each other, but she spent most of the night with someone else. Why?"

Looking over Mark's shoulder, Kendrick nodded. "They left together. Or rather, she left and they followed behind her."

"Who is she?" John asked.

Phaedra cut an eye toward Kamaya. "It's Mali Kasam. It's Daniel Kasam's daughter."

"Is she important?" Donovan asked.

"Something's up with that girl, and her father," Kamaya said. "We just don't know what that is."

"So, now that we know Mali is still here and that her father is hiding something, what's the game plan?" Phaedra asked, looking toward John.

The man hesitated for a brief moment. "I hope you girls brought your dancing shoes because I'm thinking that we're all going clubbing tonight."

Kamaya grinned. "Sleazy nightclubs! You gotta love 'em!"

Kendrick leaned to whisper in Guy's ear. His brother nodded his agreement.

"Under the circumstances I'm thinking that we shouldn't go back unarmed," Kendrick said out loud, looking around the room.

Phaedra raised an eyebrow. She wanted to ask about the legality of having a weapon in Thailand, but she didn't. She looked at John, who gave her a slight wink.

"We'll head to Mason's and get what we need. I have a key to the gun case," Guy said.

Phaedra's mouth fell open. "Mason has a gun case? With guns?" she asked.

Kamaya laughed. "Our brother is quite the marksman," she said. "Besides, tourist Thailand is quite different from underground Thailand. There are places here that can be quite dangerous if you're not careful. We learned that when Mason began building this property."

"Only because you didn't know how to stay put when we told you to," Kendrick said.

Kamaya shrugged. "Sometimes a girl has to do what a girl has to do. Isn't that right, Phaedra?"

Without giving it a second thought, Phaedra nodded with conviction. "Yeah, so you boys better get a good nap because tonight we're going to get some answers. I don't care what it takes, but we're going to find Mason and bring him home."

As Phaedra and Kamaya exited the room, strategizing in hushed whispers, John, Matthew and Mark all shook their heads, the other men chuckling softly.

Phaedra had retreated to the lobby of the hotel to regroup. She wasn't accustomed to the madness of so many family members in one place at the same time. Despite the severity of the situation and the resulting stress, they still found things to laugh about, humor easing their tension. It was too much and she found herself needing a moment of quiet to reflect.

When she'd been gone for a good length of time, each of the brothers sought her out, varying degrees of concern coming in a revolving door of Stallion men. John came first, his eyes skating around the space until he saw her sitting alone in the corner.

Taking the seat beside her, he took a deep breath, saying nothing as the two of them sat side by side watching the cast of characters that paraded in and out of the hotel.

"Are you going to be okay?" John finally asked, still staring out into space.

Phaedra shrugged. "I will be once we get Mason back."

"You two have become close since you've been here."

She tossed him a quick glance. "I care about him. He's a good man. I haven't known a lot of good men."

John paused, reflecting on her comment. "I hope we can change that," he said softly.

Phaedra turned to look at John, who was looking back at her. She took a deep breath. "Your father was a good man, too, wasn't he?"

John smiled. "One of the best. You would have liked him. And I know he would have liked you, too."

Phaedra swiped at a tear that managed to escape past her thick lashes. She swallowed hard, taking a deep breath.

John reached a hand out and patted her on the back. "When we get back to Dallas I look forward to telling you more about him," he said.

She smiled. "I'd like that."

Within minutes of John's departure, Mark lumbered across the lobby, pausing when he saw her sitting alone. He moved to her side and dropped down onto an upholstered seat across from where she was sitting. He leaned forward, meeting her curious gaze.

"What's up?" Mark questioned.

Phaedra shrugged. "I'm good."

He nodded. "You need anything?"

She shook her head. "No, I'm fine. But thanks for asking."

"Okay, then, but you know that if you need anything you just have to ask, right?"

Phaedra smiled. "I appreciate that."

Mark smiled back. "But ask John. He's better at things like that."

Phaedra chuckled softly as Mark trudged back across the lobby floor, heading out the doors to the outside.

Just as Phaedra was thinking about returning to the family's suite, Matthew waved at her from the other side of the room. Rising from her seat, she headed in his direction, waiting as he and the hotel's concierge had a brief conversation.

"Are you doing okay?" Matthew asked, turning his attention back to her.

"Yes, thank you," she said.

"We're all worried about you."

"Mason's the one we need to worry about," she responded.

Matthew nodded. "My brother-in-law's tough. I'm sure he'll be fine. And I know he wouldn't want you to worry."

Phaedra shrugged. "I can't help myself."

"I just spoke to Katrina and she asked about you."

"Your wife is very sweet. You're a lucky man."

Matthew grinned. "Yeah, I am. And so is Mason," he said, giving her a quick wink.

Phaedra nodded. "I guess I need to head back up," she said.

Matthew nodded as he studied her expression. He

reached to give her a hug, wrapping his arms tightly around her. "Family can be a good thing, Phaedra," he said. "Even one you didn't expect to have. Lean on us and Mason's family, too. I promise, we won't fail you or him."

Chapter 18

Daniel was furious, rage gleaming from his eyes as if he'd gone stark, raving mad. His shouts vacillated between English and Siamese, as if his screaming in two languages would better get his message across.

But Mali was apathetic, her expression blank as she focused on a spot on the wall behind her father's head. As she chomped on her signature piece of chewing gum, her father's tirade went in one ear and out the other, the young woman clearly not concerned with his unhappiness.

"I told you to go to London. Why are you here?" Daniel screamed for the second time. "Why can you not do what I tell you to do, Mali?"

Mali sighed, her mouth pushed out in a childish pout. "I wanted to be close to Mason. He might have needed me. Those goons of yours, they hurt him," she said, snarling at the duo who stood in the doorway, waiting for their employer's next order. "They should not have hit him like they did!" she said emphatically.

Her father shook his head. "They will do what is necessary and right now they are spending far too much time babysitting you."

Daniel paused as he crossed over to the bar and poured himself a jigger of bourbon. After tossing back the first shot and pouring another, he turned his attention back to his daughter. "Now, Mason's family has come and they are asking questions. They cannot find you here, Mali. I want you out of Thailand tonight."

His daughter rolled her eyes. She rose from her seat and moved to the man's side, wrapping her arms around his waist as she pressed her head against her father's chest. "Don't be angry with me, Papa! I hate when you yell!"

"You make me yell. You know how important this is. I need this money!"

Mali shrugged. "And you will get your money. And when I rescue Mason it will all be perfect. That's why I have to be here, Papa, so that I can rescue him and he will know how important he is to me."

Daniel stared at his daughter intently. Mali was spoiled beyond reason and he had no one to blame except himself. Mali's mother had died in childbirth and his precious baby girl had been all he'd had left. Giving her everything she wanted had made her unreasonable and selfish and had finally taxed him into financial ruin. Hoping to scam money for holding Mason hostage was his last hope to turn his and Mali's lives around.

There had been a time when he had hoped Mason would have loved Mali as much as he did, the two partnering as in-laws. But Mali's disregard for other people and her constant tantrums had done nothing to inspire the man to want a relationship with her. Mali's shameless pursuit had turned Mason off, and as much as Daniel loved his only child he hadn't been able to blame the man for his disinterest. Even at her very best Mali could frustrate a person senseless.

He shook his head, his tone hardening. "There is much more at stake here, Mali. Without that money we will lose everything. When we have that money, then I will decide what we do with Mason Boudreaux. Now, do what I ask, please."

Mali bristled in defiance as her father stormed out of the room, his two flunkies following on his heels. She stole a quick glance at the watch on her wrist. Grabbing her purse, she headed in the direction of the front door. Her father knew her better than anyone, and he knew that Mali did what Mali wanted. No more and no less. And in that moment, all Mali wanted was to ensure that no one and nothing came between her and her want of Mason Boudreaux.

Timing was going to be the key to their success, Phaedra thought, sipping on a glass of cola. Donovan was sitting beside her, his eyes skating around the room. They had all been in the club for over an hour, hoping against all odds that the two men who'd taken Mason, or Mali Kasam herself, would show.

The Stallion brothers were seated at a table in the back of the club, three Thai dancers vying for their attention. Guy and Kendrick were both at the bar with Kamaya, everyone pretending to be interested in nothing but a good time. The music was loud, the *thump, thump, thump* of a 1970s playlist vibrating around the room. Any other time or place Phaedra would have been enjoying herself, but in that moment she was nervous, believing that they were running out of time to get Mason back safe and sound.

As if reading her mind, Donovan said, "He's going to be fine." He met Phaedra's anxious stare.

Phaedra nodded. "I just hate that we can't get any help. The police have been useless. We're just running on instinct and what if we're wrong about the Kasams? What if we're looking in the wrong direction and something happens to Mason? I'll never be able to forgive myself."

"Let me tell you a story about my brother," Donovan started, his voice a loud whisper. "Him being the oldest of nine kids, with a father in the military and on deployment as often as he was home, put a lot of responsibility on Mason. I was only six or seven when I realized just how much pressure being the oldest had on him. He was trying to help our mother and be a surrogate father, big brother and best friend rolled up into one. And one day I asked him why he did so much. What made him want to work so hard?

"Mason said that our father told him to follow his gut instincts and always do what felt right for him to do. It's a philosophy that Mason continues to live by. He was barely out of college when he decided that he wanted to go into the hotel business and build an empire. And he sold that empire because he said the timing just felt right. He knew that there was something else in this world that he was supposed to be doing. Mason has always stepped out on faith, trusted in God and succeeded."

Donovan paused as he took a quick sip of his own

drink. "Did he tell you that he called me the night he met you?" the man asked.

Phaedra shook her head. "No, he didn't."

"Well, he did and I haven't heard him that excited in a long time and all because this beautiful woman took his picture and made him smile. And something about you and that moment felt right. His instincts told him that you were special, and Mason always trusts that gut feeling. And I tell you all this to say, trust those instincts. Mason trusted his when he followed you here. Trust yours and help us get him back. If you don't feel right about the Kasams, then there's a reason."

"Thank you," Phaedra said, pausing to reflect on his words.

With a wink, Donovan resumed his watch, his gaze skating back around the room. Phaedra saw them first, Mali entering the room behind the two thugs. The men headed to a table on the other side of the large room as their companion headed straight to the dance floor. Turning an about-face, Phaedra leaned to whisper into Donovan's ear, "As soon as I start talking with her you need to get up and leave. Don't let her catch up to you. She needs to think that you are Mason."

Donovan nodded. "No problem. I'll be in the alley with the car. As soon as she bolts we'll be right behind her."

Phaedra smiled. "Dear God, please let this work," she whispered as she gestured for Kamaya's attention. Kamaya, who'd been eyeing them intently, nodded as Phaedra gave her a thumbs-up.

Rising from her barstool, Kamaya made her way to where the two kidnappers sat, both men having distanced themselves from Mali. She sauntered easily in a seductive red dress, her hips swaying in invitation as she took a seat beside them, gesturing for a waiter to bring them each a round of drinks. It took no time at all before they were both completely entranced by the beautiful woman before them. With her coquettish laughter and overt seduction, Kamaya was like a black widow spider luring her prey.

Mark had made his way to the dance floor, his large palms resting easily against the line of Mali's narrow hips. She was dancing seductively, her head tossed back against her thin neck as she laughed, clearly amused by the attention the handsome man was showing her. Mali thrived on attention and Phaedra and Kamaya both had banked on her wanting to be the object of some man's desire before her night was done. Mark was the perfect man for the job.

When Kamaya gestured for a second round of drinks, Phaedra watched as the bartender slid two of the glasses toward Guy, the brother dropping two small white pills into the amber-colored liquor. If anyone had been paying attention, they would have noticed Kendrick slipping money into the bartender's palm and then the waitress's just before she delivered the drug-laced drinks to their intended targets.

Phaedra closed her eyes and took a deep breath. Opening them again, she watched as Frick and Frack both gulped their spirits, the duo spurred on by Kamaya's encouragement. Kendrick had assured her the drug's effects would be minimal, the two not remembering anything once they recovered. With no color, smell or taste, neither man would even be able to tell that anything at all had happened to him. They would both soon become weak and confused, or even pass out so they wouldn't be a threat to the next phase of the family's plan to rescue Mason. In the morning they'd have one hell of a headache for their indiscretions.

John crossed the room, headed in the direction of the door. As he passed Kamaya's table, he purposely bumped into the shorter of the companions. As he apologized profusely, offering to buy them all another round of drinks, there was no way not to notice the man's clear lack of focus, his head rolling awkwardly. Evenutally he laid his head on the table, appearing to fall off to sleep. Kamaya turned to Phaedra and winked, her head bobbing against her shoulders.

"Wish me luck," Phaedra said as Donovan gave her hand a quick squeeze before purposely pushing his full glass of drink into her lap. Phaedra jumped to her feet, squealing loudly enough to draw everyone's attention. She brushed at the offending moisture, her head shaking as Donovan pretended to assist her. Spinning away from the table, Phaedra crossed the room still muttering profusely as she headed past the dance floor toward the restrooms.

Mark was laughing as he pointed in her direction. Mali turned to stare where he stared, her eyes widening as she noticed the man who was following Phaedra with his eyes. Her gyrations came to a fast halt, her heart suddenly beating with a vengeance. How was such a thing possible? she thought, her mind suddenly spinning with questions, unable to fathom how Mason had managed to free himself. Unable to fathom how she was going to explain that to her father.

"Mali!" Phaedra cried as she suddenly blocked the woman's view. "What a surprise!" Phaedra leaned to give the girl a hug, then extended her hand in Mark's direction. "Hi, Phaedra Parrish. I'm a friend of Mali's."

Mark nodded politely. "Looks like you had a little accident," he said as he pointed to the spill down the front of her dress.

Phaedra shrugged. "My boyfriend, Mason, was a little clumsy," she said as she turned to point in Donovan's direction.

"Mason is here?" Mali questioned, unable to hide the look of surprise across her face.

"Yes," Phaedra said, a brilliant smile painting her expression. She shifted her body to block Mali's view a second time. "I know you heard about him disappearing, but he was able to get away and we're celebrating. We're leaving tomorrow, though, so we can put all of this bad business behind us."

Mali shook her head as she made a motion to move. Mark caught her about the waist. "Don't you want to keep dancing, pretty lady?" he said sweetly.

Mali brushed him off. "I need to say hello to my friend," she said as she moved to step past Phaedra.

Mark grabbed her by the arm and swung her back against him. "But we're having such a good time!" he said excitedly.

As Mali pushed him from her, snatching her arm from his grip, she didn't notice that Donovan had risen from his seat and was exiting the club, the man stealing out of the spotlight he'd been placed in. Kamaya, Kendrick and Guy followed closely behind him.

As the door closed on their departure, Phaedra cut a quick eye in Mark's direction. "Well, it was good to see you, Mali," she said, still swiping at the wet spot that had darkened the silk print she wore. "Please give your father my regards."

Before Phaedra's last words were out, Mali was searching the room, frantic to spy the man who looked like Mason Boudreaux. As she rushed in the direction of the club's entrance, she shouted in Siamese to the two men who'd arrived with her, both sitting alone, heads bowed as they slumbered comfortably at their table. Not bothering to wait for them, Mali rushed outside.

John stood at the door's entrance, blocking her quick exit. "Excuse me," he said as he stepped left when she stepped right, and right as she went left, the two looking as if they might be dancing.

"Get out of my way!" Mali shouted, clearly perturbed.

"I really am sorry," John said, feigning an apology. He stepped out of her way to allow her to pass.

Rushing past him, Mali looked left and then right, and the only thing in her view was the empty street.

Chapter 19

"Don't lose her," Kamaya said as Donovan maneuvered the car through the dark Thai streets.

"I'm not going to lose her," he responded, annoyance on the tip of his tongue. "You need to relax."

From the backseat, Guy and Kendrick admonished them both. "Stay focused," Guy said, Kendrick echoing his sentiments.

Ahead of them Mali was racing her car as if she were late for an important meeting. Just as Phaedra and Kamaya had both predicted, the combination of alcohol and dim light had successfully deceived her. Seeing Mason's brother had thrown her for a loop; the woman had lost control. After exiting the nightclub she'd headed straight for her vehicle, not bothering to wait for her two bodyguards. Anticipating that they were following close behind her, Mali didn't give the car in her rearview mirror a second thought. And both families were banking on her negligence, hopeful that she would lead them directly to where Mason was being held. The one unknown in their plan was whether or not they'd be able to rescue him without incident. And everyone was hoping that wherever Mason was, the area would be secluded, with little interference to get in their way.

In the vehicle behind them, John navigated at a safe distance, not wanting to draw any attention to the fact that there were actually two cars in hot pursuit of the young woman. Mark rode shotgun, one hand gripping the dashboard. Phaedra and Matthew held court in the backseat.

"I don't have a plan from here," Phaedra said, her eyes skipping from the back of John's head to Mark's.

"The plan is that you are going to sit in the car and stay out of the way," Mark said. He looked to the backseat.

"You are not the boss of me," Phaedra shouted, bristling with indignation.

"I didn't say I was the boss of you, but you need to listen. Why are you being difficult?"

"I'm not being difficult," Phaedra countered. "Why are you?"

John cast a quick glance in the rearview mirror, meeting Matthew's amused stare. The two brothers chuckled softly to themselves.

"I'm the boss of everybody," John said, "and you two need to play nice."

Annoyed, both Mark and Phaedra fell into the silence, sulking in their seats. Matthew laughed out loud, and Phaedra, who was totally perturbed, punched him in the arm.

"Ouch! What did you do that for?" Matthew cried out as he rubbed the rising bruise.

Phaedra rolled her eyes. "It's his fault," she said, pointing at Mark.

"Apologize, Phaedra," John said. "I don't care whose fault it is."

Phaedra bit her bottom lip, crossing her arms over her chest.

"Now," John admonished. "Say you're sorry."

She took a deep breath. "Sorry, Matthew."

For a brief moment a blanket of silence dropped down over them and then all four burst out laughing, the moment alleviating the stress that was fighting to consume them.

Mali fumbled with the key to the master lock that secured the door to the storage shed. Frustration was clouding her view, her anxiety obscuring every ounce of rational thought. There was no way Mason had gotten out, she thought, but how else would that explain how the man had found his way to Club Pattaya to spill a drink on Phaedra's dress?

Pushing open the door, she flicked on the oversize flashlight, shining it inside. Mason lay on the bed, his back to the door, exactly where he'd been the last time she looked in on him. Nothing had changed; even the food her father had left for him was undisturbed. She rubbed her hand across her eyes, swiping at the perspiration that had risen over her brow. Taking a deep breath, she held it as she eased her way inside the small enclosure, the heels of her Chanel pumps clicking loudly against the cement floor.

Shining the light on Mason, she leaned over his

body, her heart beating rapidly as she waited to see
him breathe, relief coming when he took a breath, his
body shifting with the exhalation. She reached a tenta-
tive hand out, brushing the backs of her fingers along
the side of his face. He was running a fever, his body
temperature spiked high. Knowing that there was no
way Mason could have been in that nightclub, realiza-
tion set in that she had been played.

A wave of anger suddenly flooded Mali's spirit.
Phaedra had played her, stringing her along like a gui-
tar player. Mali didn't take kindly to anyone besting
her, and she was suddenly outraged, determined to get
revenge. Spinning about on her high heels, she turned
just as Mason rolled onto his back, lifting his head to
stare at her. He brought his hand up to shield his eyes
from the light, squinting to focus.

His voice was low and craggy, the fever evident in
his tone, delirium blanketing his perception. "Phaedra?
Is that you, baby? Phaedra, are you okay?" he asked
as he tried to sit up.

Turning to stare at him, Mali grimaced, unable to
hide her dismay. He was calling Phaedra's name, and
not hers, and that made her even angrier. It was on the
tip of her tongue to cuss him, but she didn't. Instead,
she switched off the light as she eased her way back-
ward to the door. And as she turned to make her exit,
Mali slammed harshly into Donovan and Guy Boudreaux, who were standing like stone in the entrance.

As she lifted her arm to swing the flashlight at his
head, Donovan grabbed the woman's wrist and pushed
her back against the wall. "I wouldn't do that if I were
you," he said as he turned the flashlight back on and

waved the light around the space, resting it on Mason's reclined frame.

Guy moved past him, rushing to his brother's side. Kamaya and Kendrick followed on his heels. Noticing the lantern, Kamaya dropped to the floor, fiddling with the wick and a pack of matches that rested beside it. In seconds, a stream of light flooded the room. "Is he okay?" she questioned, concern spilling past her lips.

"We need to get him to a doctor," Guy said. "He's burning up and it looks like he might have lost a good amount of blood." He pointed to the stained mattress beneath his brother's head.

Kendrick called his name. "Mason...can you hear me?"

Mason struggled to focus. "Who...I..." he sputtered softly, his eyes closing as he fell back into a stupor.

"I found him," Mali said loudly. "I was trying to save him. I was just going to call for help. I wouldn't let anything happen to Mason!"

"We need to move," Donovan said, ignoring her. "Get him to the car."

With Kendrick bracing his brother's weight on one side and Guy on the other, the two lifted Mason to his feet.

"Everything is going to be fine now, Mason," Kamaya said, bringing up the rear. "We've got you, big brother."

They heard him just seconds before they saw him enter the room. He spoke in Siamese, his words meant only for his daughter's ears. As Daniel Kasam stepped into the room, he fired into the midnight air, the gunshot ringing loudly. They all came to a standstill in anticipation of a second shot, panic blowing through the space as the man pointed a large gun squarely at Mason's heart.

The silence was thundering. Donovan released his hold on Mali, the woman pushing him harshly in the chest as she moved to stand beside her father. Daniel was not amused by the smirk on her face, his daughter sneering as if everything was going to be okay.

"I am very sorry for this," he said, looking from one Boudreaux to the other. "This was not how things were supposed to go. You were supposed to pay the money and we would have let him go."

"So, what now?" Donovan questioned, easing himself slowly in front of Kamaya. "Do you plan to shoot us all, Daniel?"

The man swiped the back of his hand across his brow. He shook his head. "I just needed the money," he said. "You don't understand."

"But we do," Guy said. "And that's not going to happen now. So the only choice you have is to kill us all or let us go."

"Don't listen to them, Papa," Mali demanded. "We can fix this. We can make them get us the money. We can—"

"Shut up, Mali!" Daniel shouted. "I have to think. If you had just done what I told you to do, we would not be in this position."

"You need to decide now," Kendrick said. "Because Mason needs a doctor and the only way we're not leaving here is if you shoot us."

"You leave when I say so," Daniel shouted back, turning the gun to point at Kendrick's head.

"Not this time," John said as he and Mark moved in behind the father and his daughter, surprising them both.

Mark pointed his own pistol to the back of Daniel's head. "You might want to put that down, friend," he said softly. "We don't want any blood to be spilled tonight."

It was a standoff and that brief moment felt like a lifetime. The silence was consuming, so harsh that every heartbeat resounded like thunder. Taking a deep breath Daniel finally acknowledged defeat as he lifted his hands, opening his palms in submission. John reached for the gun Daniel was holding, pulling the firearm from the man's hand. "In the corner," he said, gesturing for Daniel and his daughter to move.

Daniel moved to the other side of the room as he and Mali both turned to stare, watching as the brothers carried Mason out the door.

Phaedra met them in the entrance, wrapping her arms around the man's waist. "Mason!"

Opening his eyes, Mason met her eyes and held the gaze for a brief moment. A slight smile pulled at his lips as he whispered her name. "Phaedra?"

Phaedra nodded. "I love you, Mason," she said as she kissed his lips, pressing her cheek to his. "I love you," she whispered before stepping out of the way so that they could get him to the car.

"We'll meet you at the hospital," Kamaya said, dropping a warm hand against Phaedra's arm. "Good job," she finished, giving Phaedra a quick wink.

Inside, Mali persisted. "What are you going to do with us?" she questioned, her eyes widening.

Phaedra pushed past the brothers, coming to a stop in front of the woman.

"I thought we told you to stay in the car," Mark admonished.

"I have some unfinished business," Phaedra said, looking at him. "And I told you, you are not the boss of me!"

"Let's go, Phaedra," John commanded. "We need to check on Mason."

"What about us?" Mali asked again, leveling her gaze on Phaedra.

Phaedra looked from her to Daniel, who'd sunk to the floor, visibly sobbing. Mali's father was broken. There was no denying the wealth of hurt that consumed him, everything he had ever valued gone with a series of bad decisions. Phaedra shook her head. "Your father needs you, Mali," she said. "You are all he has."

Mali sneered, twisting her mouth to sound off. A torrent of expletives flew past her lips, but before she could get the second wave out, Phaedra balled up a tight fist and busted the girl in the mouth. Mali fell back in surprise, landing flat on her behind on the floor beneath her. "And if you come anywhere near me or my man ever again, I will hurt you," Phaedra said, her index finger waving erratically.

"Damn!" Mark shouted as he pulled his own fist to his mouth. "Nice right cross!"

John shook his head. "Phaedra, move it. Now!"

Mason was diagnosed with a concussion, heatstroke and severe dehydration. After a day of intravenous fluids and some serious bed rest, the doctors at the Phuket International Hospital released him. Back at the hotel, both Kamaya and Phaedra were smothering him with attention.

"Girls, I'm not handicapped," Mason said, admonishing them both to give him a break.

"You better enjoy this," Kamaya said. "It won't last much longer 'cause we're leaving this afternoon."

"Uh, pay your sister no mind," Phaedra said, smiling. "I'm not going anywhere."

"Don't be bringing him into any bad habits," Kamaya teased. "You'll regret it once he gets better."

The men in the room all laughed. "I could use a cool drink of something," Mark quipped, "in case one of you would like to wait on me hand and foot."

Phaedra rolled her eyes. "Uh, you've got two good hands." She looked at Mark as he eyed her back.

Matthew laughed. "Y'all two are funny."

Mason chuckled softly. He turned his attention to John. "So, what's happening with Daniel?"

John shrugged. "Officer Niran took him and Mali both into custody, but it seems that they have a long history between them. I don't anticipate that much will come of it. He's actually charged the two men who took Mason with assault to cause bodily harm and detaining by force. They'll see more time than Daniel will."

"Daniel called me," Mason said, the pronouncement surprising them all. "He called to apologize."

"He's got some nerve," Kamaya said. "He kidnaps you, demands one million dollars in ransom and he thinks all he has to do is apologize?"

Mason shrugged. "Desperate times will make people do desperate things, Kamaya. I can't discount that without Daniel's help I would not have been able to accomplish half of what I accomplished here in Thailand. Daniel is not a bad man. He just made a very bad decision. In his eyes one million dollars wouldn't make a dent in my bank account, so it wasn't going to be missed."

"That she-devil he calls a daughter isn't much help to him, either," Phaedra muttered under her breath.

Mason smiled, pulling the woman's hand to his lips as he kissed her palm. "Mali has some issues, there's no denying that."

"Some issues?" she repeated, pulling her hand to her hip as she stared down at him.

Mason lifted his hands as if in surrender, laughing warmly. "Sorry, sensitive subject."

"Watch her right cross," Mark teased. "Mali found out the hard way that Phaedra packs a mean punch."

Phaedra flipped her hand at Mark, moving to take the seat at Mason's side.

"So, you're not going to do anything about him?" Kamaya persisted.

Mason sighed. "If he accepts it, I'm going to extend a helping hand both emotionally and financially to help him get back on his feet."

"You're crazy!" his sister yelled, throwing her hands up in frustration.

"Maybe, but sometimes we have to remember that our good fortune isn't everyone else's good fortune. As a family we have each other to lean on for support. We have an excess of financial security. Our blessings have been plentiful. Sometimes we have to look past people's mistakes and focus on their needs."

Kamaya rolled her eyes. "Yeah, yeah, yeah," she said, tears misting her eyes.

Phaedra nodded her understanding as she met John's gaze.

John came to his feet. "Mason, we're going to give you and your family some time together. If you don't mind, my brothers and I would like to steal Phaedra away from you for a minute or two."

He locked eyes with Phaedra and smiled warmly. A twinge of anxiety wafted through her stomach. She took a deep breath as Mason squeezed her hand.

"She'll be in good hands," Matthew interjected.

Mason nodded. "Be easy with my girl," he said softly. He leaned to kiss her cheek.

Meeting Mason's gaze one last time, Phaedra followed the Stallion men out of the hotel suite and down the hall. Matthew used a security pass to open the door to the second suite that the two families had been sharing. John led the way to the outside patio, taking a seat in one of the cushioned chairs. He gestured for Phaedra to follow, four chairs pulled up into a tight circle.

As Matthew sat down he pulled a sealed envelope from out of his breast pocket, passing the mailer to his older brother. Leaning forward in his seat, John rested his elbows against his thighs, flipping the envelope over in his hands. Phaedra took a deep breath. She twisted her hands nervously in her lap, suddenly wishing that she was still sitting by Mason's side, leaning on the man for support.

John started the conversation. "We've all been anxious to get the paternity results, and they came shortly after we left Texas. I asked the office to express them here to us and with everything that's been going on we really haven't had any time to review them."

"What about Luke?" Phaedra asked, her voice a hushed whisper.

"We'll share the news with him when he gets back from his honeymoon, but it's not fair to you to wait any longer."

John looked from Matthew to Mark as he passed the envelope in his hand to Phaedra. She took it tentatively, her hand visibly shaking. Tears misted behind her eyelids. Just as she slid her thumb beneath the sealed edge, Mark stopped her, dropping his own hand over hers. He shook his head. Phaedra eyed him curiously as he pulled the envelope from her grasp.

Meeting John's stare, Mark tore the envelope and its contents in half. Moving back inside the lavish hotel room, he returned with an empty trash can. Pulling a lighter from his pocket, he ignited the corner of the paper and once it was lit dropped the two halves of the flaming paper into the canister. The family sat in silence as they watched the document burn until nothing but gray ash remained.

Phaedra turned to stare at Mark. "Why—" she started, the words catching deep in her heart.

"Because I don't need that piece of paper to tell me who my family is," Mark said, casually shrugging.

John and Matthew both smiled widely. John nodded. He stood up, extending an outstretched hand. Matthew stood with him, dropping his hand atop John's. Mark added his to the mix, the three brothers turning to stare at Phaedra.

"What are you waiting for, little sis?" Mark asked.

Phaedra looked from one to the other, her tears beginning to seep past her lashes.

"She's crying," Mark said, his eyes spinning skyward. "And she's doing that ugly cry that Luke used to do."

"Sisters cry, little brother," John replied with a slight chuckle. He nodded his head at Phaedra. "So, what are you waiting for?" he asked a second time.

Coming to her feet, Phaedra dropped her hand on top of the pile. John placed his other hand on top of hers, squeezing it warmly. The others followed until they were all hands in.

"Welcome to the family," Mark said softly, tossing her a wink.

"Once a Stallion," Matthew chimed in.

"Forever a Stallion," John and Mark echoed.

"Once a Stallion," Matthew repeated, his gaze meeting Phaedra's, his eyebrows raised.

The three brothers all grinned at Phaedra.

"Forever a Stallion," she answered, knowing that from that moment forward, those words would always be true.

Chapter 20

"So, you two are headed where?" Mark questioned, his eyes narrowing suspiciously.

Mason laughed. "I'm thinking that we might fly to Greece before we head back to the States."

"And how long do you plan to be in Greece?"

"One, maybe two days."

Mark nodded, his expression moving Phaedra to laugh.

"Why are you giving Mason the third degree?" she asked.

Mark looked at her. "It's what big brothers do," he answered.

Matthew and John both laughed heartily. The two leaned to kiss Phaedra's cheek.

"You're coming back to Dallas after Greece, right, Phaedra?" John asked.

Phaedra nodded. "I need to stop in N'Orleans first, but yes, I'm coming back to Dallas."

"We'll talk more then," he said as he gestured for his brothers to get on the Stallion jet. "Let's move it," he said, heading in the direction of the private plane.

Mark moved to Phaedra's side, wrapping her in a deep hug. He met Mason's amused gaze over the woman's shoulder. "Take care of my little sister," he said sternly. "I think we're going to keep her."

Mason laughed, giving the man a quick salute. "Yes, sir."

Mark laughed with him as the duo slapped palms.

Phaedra stepped into Mason's arms as they watched the siblings board their plane for home.

"Greece?" Phaedra said as Mason led her by the hand to his own private aircraft.

"Would you prefer Italy? We can go wherever you want to go."

"You're killing me," she said, giggling softly.

"With love, baby. Just with love!"

Phaedra reached to kiss Mason's lips. "In all honesty, what I would like to do is just go to N'Orleans. After everything that's happened I need something familiar. I really just want to go home."

Mason nodded his understanding. "Then we're going home," he said.

An hour later the pilot confirmed the change in their travel itinerary and the duo was on their way back to the United States. As the Gulfstream G450 ascended into the midday sky, Phaedra blew a sigh of relief, grateful that she was still standing because for the past month all she had wanted to do was lie down and pull the covers over her head.

Since her mother's death, every aspect of her life had felt like something out of a novel, feeling unbelievable. She'd gone from having no family to having four brothers, and a man who loved her and talked about spending the rest of his life with her. The week before she'd been pointing a camera at pretty things taking pictures, and just days earlier she'd witnessed guns being pointed at people she loved, threatening to take their lives. She'd traveled from New Orleans to Dallas in economy class to Thailand on a private jet, and with Mason the next stop would be wherever her heart desired, by whatever mode of travel she wanted.

She'd had to make life-changing decisions on the fly, and just days after her mother's passing a grief counselor had warned her not to make any major resolutions for at least six months. She'd been blessed beyond measure, but she couldn't stop thinking that all of it was just a phenomenal dream and she would soon wake up from it.

"A penny for your thoughts," Mason said, his fingers gliding down the length of her arm.

Phaedra shook her head. "You really don't want to know what I was thinking."

"Yes, I do. I don't want you to think that you ever have to keep anything from me. And right now you look like your world has just fallen apart. I don't like that look and if I can do something to take that kind of worry from your heart I want to do it," Mason said.

"I guess I was just worried that my world might want to fall apart," Phaedra answered. "A lot has happened and I keep waiting for the other shoe to drop."

Mason nodded, his expression reflective. "Do you believe that good things come to good people, Phaedra?"

"Sometimes."

"Maybe this is your sometime. Maybe your blessings are coming because you are deserving of them."

Phaedra shook her head. "How are you such an optimist?"

"How are you not?"

Mason leaned to kiss her, his hand cupped gently against the side of her face. His lips were soft and teasing, stirring a rumbling of heat in the center of her core. The last time they'd made love had been the morning Mason had been taken, and Phaedra admitted to having been scared that he would never make love to her again.

Mason broke the connection, staring into her eyes as he pulled himself away. He took a deep breath, a wry smile pulling at his mouth.

"What?" Phaedra asked, smiling with him.

He leaned to whisper in her ear, stealing a glance toward the galley to ensure that they didn't have an audience. "I'm hard," he said, brushing his face gently against hers. "Every time I think about you I get an erection and we haven't had a moment alone," he whispered.

Phaedra laughed. "That sounds like a deeply personal problem, Mr. Boudreaux."

Mason nodded. "It will be if I have to spend the next sixteen hours in this airplane, excited, without getting any relief."

Still giggling, Phaedra pointed to the plane's restroom. "You might want to go take care of that problem," she said.

Mason grinned. "I didn't think you'd ever ask," he said, rising from his seat. He grabbed Phaedra's hand and pulled her along behind him.

Her eyes widened in surprise. "What...I..." she sputtered as he pulled her into the bathroom and locked the door. "Mason!" Phaedra cried out. "We can't—"

Before she could complete the thought, Mason pulled her into his arms and kissed her hungrily, his mouth consuming hers. When he licked the fullness of her lips, moving her to open her mouth to him, his tongue danced past the line of her teeth, swirling in sync with hers. He pressed his body against her, Phaedra's softness cushioning every one of his hardened muscles.

"Well, maybe this one time," Phaedra purred as Mason nuzzled his face into her neck, planting a line of kisses from one ear to the other. She shivered in ecstasy as Mason painted circles with his tongue across the soft, supple skin of her neck. Phaedra closed her eyes and lost herself in the delicious feelings swirling through her. Heat rose with a vengeance in the small enclosure, perspiration rising fiercely in every crack and crevice of both their bodies.

Mason teased her for what seemed like an eternity. Phaedra moaned as Mason's lips and tongue danced sensually against her blazing skin. She felt as if she could collapse from the intense pleasure.

"Take this off," Mason ordered as he tugged at the bottom of Phaedra's blouse. He twisted the buttons and she slipped off the silky material. As Mason hung it over the door handle, Phaedra unlatched her bra, releasing her breasts. Her firm chocolate nipples stood at attention.

"Mmm," Mason whispered as he captured one rock-hard candy in his mouth, his thumb and forefinger pulling at the other.

"Ohhh," Phaedra gasped, sucking in air at the intense sensation, shivering as Mason teased her sensitive flesh. Every ounce of sensibility was gone from her, the woman barely able to remember her own name as she focused on the sensations sweeping through her body. Mason's tongue flicked and teased her as he sucked hard on the sweet gem, sending sparks of heat deep into her feminine core. Phaedra sighed in ecstasy as her body began to shake and her moans intensified.

Wanting him to feel what she was feeling, Phaedra glided her palm down the front of his chest to his belt and unbuckled it. Before Mason realized it she had eased his zipper down and was sliding her palm over his crotch, the heat from her hands igniting a firestorm in his erection. He was brick-hard, the length of his manhood pulsing for release. Mason inhaled swiftly, humming as Phaedra began to stroke him earnestly. Suddenly Phaedra stopped cold and Mason shuddered, his body quivering for more. He looked at her, his desire washing over his expression.

"Drop your pants," she said.

Mason smiled as he let his pants and boxers slide down to the floor, releasing the protrusion of flesh that was desperate for her ministrations. She grasped him firmly in both hands, manipulating him with an intensity that had him fighting to stand, his knees threatening to buckle beneath him. Mason still had a firm grasp on her breasts, his mouth and tongue continuing to tease her.

"I need you," Mason whispered. "I need to be inside you," he gushed, his hips pumping in time with her strokes.

Phaedra kissed him again, the passion of it consuming them both. Mason suddenly spun her toward the sink and mirror, looping his arm around her waist. He pulled her to his chest, gently biting the back of her neck. Phaedra sank into him as he cradled his pelvis against the round of her bottom, grinding heavily against her. Pulling at her pants, Mason snatched them from her around her buttocks, his hands eagerly stroking the softness between her thighs. Stepping out of her G-string, Phaedra parted her legs, moving eagerly against his fingers.

As Mason bent her forward, Phaedra braced herself against the pedestal sink, holding tightly as Mason entered her from behind. His strokes were urgent and searching, driving her to a level of ecstasy that she had not known was possible. She bit down against her bottom lip to keep from crying out loudly, the sweet sensations drawing every ounce of breath from her.

Mason hugged her to him, his arms tight around her torso, one hand still stroking each nipple as Phaedra drew the fingers of his other hand into her mouth and sucked the appendages with vigor. His pelvis pushed and pulled against her, her bottom colliding into him with each stroke, and then with an intensity that rocked every nerve ending the two of them exploded together, their orgasms erupting in one tumultuous wave after another.

Collapsing against her back, Mason was panting, fighting to catch his breath. Phaedra was breathing heavily as well, her body still twitching with pleasure. Minutes later, their clothes adjusted back onto their bodies, the two of them eased their way out of the restroom. Returning to their seats, they strapped themselves back in, holding tight to each other's hand.

Outside, the plane seemed to be floating on a snow-white cushion of thick clouds. Peering out the window, Phaedra leaned her head against Mason's chest as he wrapped his arms tightly around her. Every ounce of doubt that had flooded her spirit earlier had dissipated into thin air. With it feeling like home in Mason's arms, the moment was heaven and Phaedra was grateful for it.

With Phaedra feeling as though all was well in the world, their landing at the Louis Armstrong New Orleans International Airport was simply the sweetest cherry on top of the best confection. Stepping out of the plane, she took a deep breath, inhaling the familiar scent of home. A limousine sat in wait at the end of the tarmac.

Phaedra shook her head. "Mason, we could have taken a taxi," she said, amazed at how he always seemed to have a pulse on what they needed before the thought even crossed her mind. "When did you arrange for a car?"

Mason shrugged. "I have a very adept staff of employees," he said as the driver opened the car door to let them inside.

"I need to meet this staff," Phaedra said.

The man smiled. "You will, and very soon, I'm sure."

Traveling through the streets, the duo compared notes, both having stories about growing up in New Orleans. Phaedra's excitement incited his, Mason seeing his hometown in a different light. The last time he'd been in the city for any length of time had been shortly after the hurricane when the shine had been considerably dimmed. The stopovers since had been quick and sweet, lasting just long enough to check on the renovations of his family's home.

When the car stopped at the quaint house on S. Claiborne Avenue, Phaedra's excitement was palpable, the woman bursting with glee as she rushed to open the front door. And Mason was excited for her, her joy like a sweet balm to his spirit. After he and the driver had gotten their luggage to the front porch, Phaedra called for him to come inside. As he entered the comfortable space, her smile was a wide explosion across her face.

"Welcome to my home," she said, her arms thrown out to her sides.

Mason laughed. "Very nice," he said, his eyes darting around the room. "This looks like you."

"It looks like my mother," she said, pointing to a photo of a woman that sat on the mahogany end table.

Mason eased his way to stand in front of the fireplace, examining the collection of family photos that decorated the mantel. Photos of Phaedra as a baby. Her high school graduation picture. Formal portraits of mother and daughter together.

Her mother had been a beautiful woman, and he told her so. "I see where you got your good looks from."

"Thank you. She would have adored you," Phaedra responded, laughter shining in her eyes.

"I'm sure she and I would have been great friends," Mason said.

Phaedra grabbed his hand. "Let me show you around," she said, guiding him through the dining area and kitchen, then to the bedrooms on the second floor.

"We'll sleep here," she said, leading him into her bedroom.

Mason smiled, his eyebrows raised mischievously. "I imagine we might not be getting much sleep," he said teasingly as he wrapped his arms around her torso and hugged her to him.

Phaedra giggled as Mason blew warm breath against the side of her neck, following the warmth with his tongue. "Are you trying to get something started, Mr. Boudreaux?" she quipped.

"Yes, ma'am. I am definitely trying to get something started. Are you going to let me?"

Phaedra giggled again. "I've never had a man in my room before. My mother would be having a fit if she knew."

"I assure you that your mother would have loved me so much that my being in your room wouldn't have been an issue."

"Mmm," Phaedra purred as Mason assaulted her mouth, kissing her voraciously, their tongues twisting wildly together.

Without a moment's hesitation Phaedra wriggled out of her slacks and top and stood in front of Mason with nothing on but her tiny black thong. Mason grabbed her by her thin waist and lifted her up onto the wooden dresser. Phaedra gasped, her arms wrapped around his neck. Her thin brown legs instinctively spread open, wrapping around his waist, and Mason licked his lips in anticipation. Guiding her movements, Mason pushed her legs up until her feet were resting on the dresser top. Spread open in all her glory, she was absolutely delicious, a sweet expectation at the ready.

"Do you have any idea what I'm going to do to you?" Mason asked.

"What?" Phaedra whispered.

The man smiled, not answering out loud as he took his index finger and teased the mound that pressed against the black triangle of fabric. He was staring in her eyes when he ripped the garment with his hands, tossing the remnants to the floor. Still staring into her eyes, Mason drew his fingers in bold strokes through the folds of her femininity, blatantly teasing her.

Phaedra inhaled swiftly, lust sweeping in bold waves through her. Every time Mason touched her she was in awe of the sensation. Every muscle in her body quivered for more.

Taking a quick glance around the room, Mason reached for a desk chair and pulled it to where she sat on the dresser. As he rested his knee against the cushioned seat, settling himself comfortably in front of her, he inhaled the sweet fragrance of her intimate scent. Phaedra's eyes widening in anticipation, he licked his index finger, sucking on it slowly. Phaedra took a deep breath and held it, her body beginning to convulse with wanting. She watched in wonder as Mason slowly slid his moist finger across her swollen nub with wanting.

Phaedra gasped. "Mason! Oh, baby."

Phaedra was on fire and when Mason placed a damp kiss against her inner thigh she thought she might combust. He started slowly, allowing her temperature to rise to an unreasonable level. As he dipped his tongue into the sweetness of her inner folds, he began to lap at her more furiously. Phaedra ran her hands over his head as her body shook with pleasure. She screamed his name, her body twisting and turning as every inch of her flesh tingled.

Savoring the intimate delicacy, Mason pushed his tongue deeper into Phaedra's private garden to savor the sweetness of her nectar. As Phaedra rode the tumultuous waves, speeding closer and closer to her orgasm, Mason pulled her to him, clamping his arms around her thighs to hold her steady. She arched her back and cried out with joy.

"Ohhh!" she screamed, locking her hands behind his head. "Don't stop! Please don't stop! Ohhh, baby!"

Mason doubled, then tripled his efforts, desperate to bring Phaedra to the explosion of a lifetime. He quickly licked his finger and slid it deep inside her. She was hot and tight and as he pushed a second and then a third finger in, Phaedra bucked hard, loving the sweet intrusion into her secret box.

She moaned, calling his name over and over again. Mason held her tight as he maintained his oral assault, lavishing long, wet strokes against her swollen button.

Phaedra screamed, her senses on overload. She raced higher and higher toward ecstasy, giving in to the wanton abandon. Suddenly Mason stroked her deeper and deeper, hitting her sweet spot until her passion crested. Phaedra bucked, her back arching as her legs locked behind his head, holding him hostage between her legs. She sobbed as he buried himself into her wetness.

"Ahhhh!" Phaedra shuddered as Mason lapped every drop of her sweet liquid. As her passion ebbed and flowed he gently stroked her damp thighs, continuing to kiss the soft, damp skin. He smiled as he felt her continue to shiver in ecstasy. Rising to his feet, he lifted her into his arms and carried her to the bed, laying her gently against the handmade quilt that decorated the bed. Lying down beside her, he curled into her warmth, the lovers drifting off into a sound sleep.

Chapter 21

Mason woke to the aroma of fresh-roasted coffee and thick bacon sizzling in a cast-iron frying pan. The smells wafting through the small bedroom were transforming, shifting him from a state of total unconsciousness to bright-eyed cognizance. Taking a deep breath, he rolled over onto his back, taking in the sight of Phaedra's childhood bedroom. The decor was an amalgamation of black-and-white photographs, remnants of college paraphernalia, trinkets from her travels and rich, lush fabrics in bright, vibrant colors. The space was warm and inviting, invoking the spirit that Mason had come to love about the beautiful woman.

Making his way into the bathroom, he tossed off the clothes he'd slept in and stepped into the shower stall, turning the water to superhot. Moisture rained down over his head and shoulders, the invigorating stream pulsing over his muscles. As he soaped his body, rinsing the suds down the drain, he was excited to start his day with Phaedra, anxious to see where they would be headed together.

As he stepped out of the shower, Phaedra knocked on the bathroom door, calling his name. "Hey there, do you want some breakfast?" she asked, peeking inside.

"Good morning," Mason said, grinning brightly.

"Good morning. I thought you might be hungry," she said as she stepped into the room and passed him a plush white towel.

"I could eat," he said as he swiped the towel across his body. "How long have you been up?"

"Not long. You were sleeping soundly, so I figured I'd let you rest."

He smiled as she reached to help him dry his back, her fingers lingering longer than necessary as she swiped her hands across his skin. She stepped in and planted a moist kiss against his back and shoulders. Turning an about-face, he wrapped his arms around her and kissed her gently, relishing the comfort of the embrace. He kissed her cheek before releasing the hold. "So, what would you like to do today?" he asked, wrapping the towel around his waist.

"Actually I really don't want to do much of anything. I have a stack of mail I need to go through, the paperwork to settle my mother's estate that needs to be completed and I need to figure out where my next photo assignment is going to be. I figured we'd just hang out for a while and then maybe head downtown later?"

Mason nodded. "Sounds like a plan. I actually have a few things I need to do, as well."

"Well, you get dressed and I'll go pour your coffee." Phaedra smiled. As she turned to walk out of the room, Mason gave her a swift pat against her backside.

Down in the kitchen the two enjoyed a breakfast of bacon, eggs, toast and coffee. Their conversation was easy and relaxed, the two enjoying each other's company. Mason asked questions about her mother and their history, enjoying the slide show of photo albums that documented them together. He sensed that Phaedra was missing her mother, and talking about the joyful times they'd shared clearly lifted her spirits.

After breakfast Phaedra retreated to her office and Mason to the screened porch that bordered the backyard. Neighbors had kept the grass cut, flowers blooming in no particular order around the perimeter of the fenced area. With his laptop resting against his knees, he accessed the home's Wi-Fi to retrieve his emails, responding to a lengthy list of messages. Turning his cell phone on for the first time since leaving for Thailand, he returned some necessary telephone calls. At some point he dozed off, a cool breeze wafting comfortably through the space. When he woke Phaedra was curled up at the opposite end of the sofa, her electronic reader resting in her hand.

He stretched his body upward and yawned. "How long have I been asleep?" he asked.

Phaedra shrugged as she answered, "Most of the afternoon. I think the time difference and jet lag finally caught up with you. Plus, you're still recovering from your trauma."

She rested her e-reader against the floor and shifted her body easily over his. Mason wrapped his arms around her as she leaned to kiss his mouth. "Ready to get out into the sunshine?"

Mason smiled as he glided his hands over her buttocks, sliding them beneath the T-shirt she wore. "I can think of something else I'd rather be doing," he said as he kissed her again.

She grinned, moving her pelvis to meet his. "Are you trying to get some again, sir?"

He lifted his eyebrows, his fingers still teasing her flesh. "Yes, ma'am."

She giggled softly as she lifted herself from the sofa, stretching out her hand to take his. Following her lead, Mason trailed after her as she led him back into the house and up the stairs, both leaving a trail of clothing behind them.

Phaedra couldn't have imagined a more romantic evening as they strolled through Woldenberg Park, enjoying the evening sunset. The sun danced across the mighty Mississippi as they strolled along the river. A procession of ships floated by on the river, and interesting sculptures dotted the landscape near the docks. As they sat on one of the many benches, a violinist stopped to serenade them, the enchanting strings setting a starry mood.

As the sun disappeared in the distance, the sky gleaming in vibrant shades of red, orange and purple, Mason led the way to the Napoleon House. Cocktails at the dimly lit, rustic bar were a quiet preamble to dinner at the restaurant Lola's, where they enjoyed a tantalizing meal of Spanish food, Mason insisting that the paella was the best he'd had since visiting Spain. The restaurant was charming and quaint with only a few tables and a strict no-reservations policy. As they'd waited for a table, Mason had held her close, his arms wrapped warmly around her.

After dinner they swung by Jackson Square and grabbed a late-night ride around the French Quarter in the back of a horse-drawn carriage. The picturesque views reminded them both of what they loved most about the exotic city, and by the time they'd found their way back to Phaedra's home, the mood was set for a night of making sweet, sweet love.

Hours later Phaedra slumbered comfortably against him, her naked body curled around his. Every so often she'd draw her fingers along the curve of his buttocks, the gentle sensation against his skin soothing. She snored ever so slightly, and listening to her breathe made him smile.

In that concrete room, delirium clouding his thoughts, he'd been afraid that he'd lost her, and the thought of her being gone from him when she had just moved into his life and heart had left him broken.

Phaedra had been fearful of them moving too fast, their relationship coming on the heels of too many obstacles. He'd been more confident about the two of them, believing that God had heard and answered his persistent prayer, blessing him with a partner who would fill the emptiness that had been his life. And the more time they spent together, the more they discovered about each other, the more convinced he was that he was right.

Phaedra shifted her body closer against his, seeking out his body heat. Her breathing shifted as she tossed one leg over his. Mason smiled into the darkness.

"Are you asleep?" she whispered, wrapping an arm around his waist.

Mason shook his head against his pillow. "No, I'm wide-awake."

"Is everything okay?"

"Perfect. I was just thinking about you. About us."

"I like us," she responded, caressing his side and abdomen. "I like us a lot."

Mason rolled onto his back. Phaedra cradled her body over his, resting her head against his chest. "Me, too," Mason said, tracing his hand along her profile.

Phaedra closed her eyes and relished the sensation of his touch. She took a deep breath, then lifted her body above his, straddling him comfortably. "So, what's next with us, Mr. Boudreaux?" she asked as she palmed his chest.

"I know what I want, Phaedra. I guess the question is, what do you want?"

Phaedra paused. She took a deep breath, blowing it slowly past her lips. "There's so much for us to consider," she said, reflecting on their two situations. "Where is business going to put you?"

"What I need to do for your brothers is going to keep me traveling for a while. I don't see myself settling down in any one place for at least the next year. Maybe two. And I'm sure you will want to spend time in Dallas getting to know your family. Have you given any consideration to moving there? Because I'm sure John is going to bring the idea up to you. I know I would."

"I've thought about commuting between here and there, but no, I hadn't thought about moving."

"It's something that you might want to consider," Mason said matter-of-factly.

Phaedra nodded. "So, where would that leave us? Will this be a long-distance relationship?"

"It doesn't have to be. Depending on our schedules, you can travel with me wherever I go or I can travel with you. Money isn't an issue for us, so you'll be afforded the opportunity to take pictures all around the world if that's what you want to do."

"Money isn't an issue for *you,* Mason. I make a comfortable living, but that's all it is, comfortable."

"No, it's not an issue for us because whatever I have, you have. Most especially after we're married."

Phaedra laughed. "And you're planning to marry me?"

"Was there any doubt?"

She paused, taking a quick moment before she responded, "In all honesty, Mason, I hadn't thought about marriage. I've just gotten used to the idea of us being a couple."

"Well, I have thought about it and I can't imagine us being together and you not being my wife. And I'm not saying we have to be married tomorrow or next week, but when it feels right and you're ready, I want to marry you. I want you to know that I am committed to our being together forever. I love you, Phaedra."

Phaedra leaned to kiss him, her lips gliding like silk against his. "I love you, too, Mason," she said as he wrapped his arms around her.

His wiggled his pelvis beneath her. "So, just how much do you love me?" he said, his voice dropping to a seductive whisper.

Phaedra squirmed against him, feeling the rise of nature that surged anxiously for her attention. She grinned widely as she stroked him with her body, his erection hardening like a rod of steel between her legs. "Let me show you," she said as she reached a hand between them, her fingers wrapping around the length of him.

Mason reached toward the nightstand and the box of condoms that rested behind the lamp. He pulled a prophylactic from the container and passed it to her. Tearing the wrapper from the rubber, she shifted her body to give herself enough room to sheathe the length of him. Mason's smile pulled ear to ear in anticipation.

Dropping her mouth down to his, she kissed him sweetly. She teased him, taunting him with anticipation as her body glided firmly against his. As Mason began to thrust himself upward, grinding his body against hers, Phaedra lifted her hips and plunged her body down against him. Mason gasped at the sensation, pleasure surging through him like a wildfire that refused to be contained.

As Mason grabbed her by her hips, guiding her motion, Phaedra rode him in earnest, propelling herself up and down against him. With the length of himself nestled nicely between her legs, Mason savored the sweet sensations, Phaedra hot and delicious around him. The feelings through his body were out of this world. Mason knew that he wouldn't last long. He could feel his orgasm slowly building as Phaedra sped up her strokes. At the point of no return, Mason pushed himself into her, hard, causing her to cry out, and a second later he felt her contracting around him as she had her own climax. Collapsing against him, Phaedra nestled into his embrace, reveling in the love that spiraled in deep swirls around them both.

Mason kissed her ardently. It was like kissing an angel, he thought, nothing else nearly as perfect. Phaedra was beautiful and delicate, graceful and lithe. As he explored her body with his hands, he was drunk with lust after what they had done and what else he planned to do before the night was over.

Chapter 22

The ringing cell phone startled them both from a sound sleep. Mason jumped and Phaedra jumped with him, her body sprawled over his. She laughed huskily. "I think that's for you," she said as she rolled to the other side of the bed, pulling a pillow over her head.

Reaching for the device that rested on the nightstand, Mason pulled it to his ear. "Hello?"

The familiar voice on the other end moved him to sit upright in the bed listening intently. Phaedra peeked up at him, curiosity pulling her awake.

"Yes, sir…yes…I…but…" Mason heaved a deep sigh. "Yes, sir, I will," he repeated as he disconnected the call. The man shook his head, a smile pulling at his mouth.

"Is everything okay?" Phaedra asked, concern rising in her tone.

"We have been summoned," Mason said with a deep sigh.

Phaedra sat up in confusion. "Summoned?"

He nodded as he threw his legs off the bed. "Don't worry, it's not as bad as it sounds. Let's get dressed," he said as he tapped her gently against her backside. "We've been invited to brunch."

An hour later, Mason was maneuvering Phaedra's Toyota Camry uptown into the 14th Ward. With her efforts to pull any information from him fruitless, she was still in the dark about who had called for them or where they were going. When he pulled past the wrought-iron gates of the Broadway Street home, she looked at him, a wave of anxiety filling the pit of her stomach. Her eyes widened.

"Is this your family's home?" she questioned, eyeing him with reservation.

Mason nodded. "Yes, it is. And my parents are here. It seems that one of my siblings couldn't keep their mouth shut and they now know about the incident in Phuket."

Phaedra laughed. "And Mom and Dad are pissed, aren't they?"

"Very!" Mason said with a deep laugh. He leaned to kiss her lips. "But meeting you is going to make them forget all about it."

She shook her head. "I wouldn't place any bets on that if I were you," she said as they stepped out of the car.

Mason's mother met them at the door, pulling the entrance open before they stepped onto the porch. Katherine Boudreaux threw her arms around Mason's body, hugging him tightly. Tears misted the older woman's eyes.

"How dare you frighten me like that, Mason?" his mother said.

Mason hugged her tightly, shaking his head in earnest. "Mom, I am fine. There was nothing for you to be frightened about."

"That's not what we heard," Mason's father said, stepping out to greet them. "To hear your brothers tell it, things were pretty sketchy 'cross dem waters. Nearly got yourself killed."

"It was not that serious," Mason said, trying to alleviate the concern. He kissed his mother's cheek before extending his hand toward his father.

Mason Boudreaux Jr. shook his son's hand and then pulled him into a hearty embrace. "It's good to see you, son."

"It's good to see you, Senior."

Mason's father tossed a look past his son's shoulder, spying Phaedra, who was standing nervously on the top step.

"Good morning, pretty lady!" Mason Senior chimed, extending his hand. "Mason Boudreaux Jr., but everyone calls me Senior," he said as he pumped Phaedra's arm up and down.

Mason looped his arm around Phaedra's waist, pulling her to him. "Mom, Senior, this is Phaedra. Phaedra, this is my mother, Katherine, and my father."

Katherine wrapped Phaedra in a warm hug. "I am thrilled to meet you," the woman said excitedly. "We've heard such nice things about you, dear!"

"Thank you," Phaedra said, a smile brightening her face. "And it's so nice to meet you both."

Still holding on to Phaedra, Katherine gestured for the two of them to follow her into the house. "That was some nasty business in Thailand. I am so glad that you both are back here safe and sound."

Phaedra smiled as Mason tried to transition the topic. "The house looks great, Mom," he said, glancing around the large living room. "Are you happy with everything?"

Katherine shrugged. "I'm not unhappy, but with you kids all over the place it still doesn't feel homey yet."

"Well, I'm sure once you two settle in, it won't take long for everyone to find their way back home," Mason said.

He and Phaedra both sat down against the upholstered settee.

His mother rested on the arm of the chair his father sat down in, wrapping her arms around the man's shoulders. "Well, Senior wants to go back to Arizona for a few months since all you kids are on that side of the country. And of course once Katrina has that baby, we'll be in Dallas for a while to help her out."

"I have to keep that grandson of mine in check. You know how teens can get," he said, referring to his daughter Katrina's oldest son. "Have you met Collin yet, Phaedra?" he asked.

She nodded. "Yes, sir. He's a wonderful young man."

The proud grandfather nodded. "That's my boy!"

Katherine slid her hands across the tops of her thighs as she stood up. "I need to go get the food ready. I hope you two are hungry," she said, looking from one to the other.

Mason nodded. "Starving," he said.

"Mrs. Boudreaux, can I give you a hand?" Phaedra asked, rising to her feet.

Katherine nodded, reaching for Phaedra's hand. "I'd love some help," she said as she pulled Phaedra in the direction of the kitchen. "It will give us some time to get to know each other while my boys catch up."

Intrigued, Phaedra tossed a glance over her shoulder. Mason winked at her as she followed behind the matriarch. His smile was canyon wide. When the two women were out of earshot, his father chastised him.

"I didn't like hearing from other folks about you getting into trouble, son. Why didn't you call me?"

Mason apologized. "I didn't want to worry you and Mom. It really wasn't that serious."

Senior raised his eyebrows, his expression voicing his disbelief. Mason smiled, his head nodding ever so slightly.

"I promise, Senior, I won't let it happen again," he said.

Satisfied, Senior leaned forward in his seat, his hands clasped together in front of him. "So, tell me about your new friend," he said, gesturing with his head toward the kitchen.

"She's incredible," Mason said, grinning broadly as he gave his father an edited version of his time with Phaedra since the two had met at the Stallion wedding. "She's the most amazing woman I have ever met," he concluded.

His father nodded. "She sounds very special. And she's been through a lot. I know your sisters haven't stopped talking about her. Kamaya and Katrina have been giving your mother an earful."

Mason shook his head, only imagining how the

women in his family had been gossiping. The two men sat in conversation for some time, catching up with each other, while in the kitchen, Phaedra was becoming acquainted with his mother. The young woman stood at the kitchen counter breaking eggs into a bowl.

"Mason's been wonderful to me," Phaedra was saying, sharing the story of how he'd been so supportive since the two had come together.

"My son is a good man," Katherine said proudly, pulling a pan of biscuits from the oven.

Phaedra smiled, nodding her agreement. By the time she helped carry the meal to the kitchen table, Katherine calling her husband and son to come eat, the two women had become fast friends. Katherine reminded her of her own mother, and Phaedra was grateful for the time with the woman, noting how much she had missed the maternal companionship.

The rest of the morning flew by, laughter ringing soundly through the home as the family enjoyed the midmorning meal. Mason's parents regaled her with stories of Mason's childhood, his many antics moving her to shake her head.

"Stop, stop!" Mason cried, holding a hand up. "Don't tell that story," he said to his father, shaking his head. "Phaedra may not like me anymore if you keep telling her these stories," he teased.

Phaedra leaned to kiss his lips. "I'm enjoying this," she said. "Definitely don't stop!"

He shook his head, everyone trying to catch their breaths from laughing so hard. Hours later, Phaedra excused herself to go to the restroom.

Katherine crossed over to her son's side and hugged him warmly.

"She's perfect for you," she intoned. "She is absolutely delightful."

Mason nodded. "I love her, Mom," he said softly. "I didn't know it was possible to love any woman the way I love Phaedra." He met his father's stare, the man smiling contently.

Katherine hugged him a second time as she whispered into his ear, "She loves you, too, but just take it slow and enjoy your time together. She's still fragile and you don't want to scare her."

Nodding his understanding, Mason grinned, joy shimmering out of his eyes over his parents' approval of his and Phaedra's relationship. Moments later Phaedra stood in the doorway, staring at the bond between the parents and their son as they sat laughing easily together. Delighting in the moment, she lifted her requisite camera to her eyes and snapped a photo, capturing the moment for her and Mason's family album.

Chapter 23

John Stallion had dispatched the limousine that picked the family up at the airport. Phaedra was feeding off their excitement, Mason and his parents bursting with elation as they headed in the direction of Dallas's new Parkland Hospital.

Matthew had called hours earlier to say that Katrina was on her way to have the baby, and with a private plane at their disposal it had taken them less than two hours to get from New Orleans to Dallas, their arrival beating the new baby's.

Mason laughed warmly. "Your brother is so excited. He sounds like he's about to bust," he said as he disconnected his cell phone. "She's still in labor. No baby yet!"

Katherine laughed. "I told Katrina that baby was going to take his dear sweet time coming here. Collin was a slow baby, remember? Katrina was in labor almost eighteen hours with him."

Mason shook his head. "If I knew it was going to take that long, we could have taken our time getting here," he said.

His father nodded in agreement.

Phaedra chuckled. "Do you think it's a boy, Mrs. Boudreaux?"

"I'm sure it's a boy. Katrina was carrying this baby low, just like Collin."

Her husband shook his head. "What you gon' do if that baby is a girl?" he asked teasingly.

Katherine tossed him a look that spoke volumes, and both the Boudreaux men burst out laughing.

At the hospital, the families were gathered in the waiting room outside the maternity ward. Their laughter could be heard down the long length of corridor. It was a Stallion-Boudreaux reunion, the likes of which Phaedra had never seen before. She smiled brightly as they rushed into the room to join in the wait.

Her brothers each greeted her warmly, hugging and kissing her easily as they exchanged dap with Mason. The Stallion women were just as welcoming, pulling her into their conversations with ease.

"Where we at?" Senior asked, his arm draped over young Collin's shoulder.

"It's close," John said as Marah stepped into his arms, hugging him around the waist.

"This is so exciting!" Kamaya said as she pulled Phaedra into the empty seat beside her and her sister Tarah, introducing them to each other and Phaedra to the other members of the Boudreaux family.

The noise was abundant and every so often, Katherine and Juanita would shush them to a low murmur. At every opportunity Phaedra snapped pictures with her camera, wanting to capture as many of the memo-

ries as she could. Time passed swiftly and before the
sun began to set outside, Matthew entered the room,
still dressed in the required scrubs expectant fathers
donned in the delivery room. Tears misted his dark
eyes, his hands wringing excitedly.

"It's a boy," he shouted. "Nine pounds two ounces!"

"It's a big boy!" Katherine said with excitement as
she and Juanita both rushed to give him a hug.

"How's Katrina?" Katherine asked, her husband
moving to wrap his arms around her waist.

"She's doing great. Tired but she's just fine."

"So, do we get to see it?" Collin asked anxiously.

Matthew laughed. "Your little brother is not an it.
And yes, you can see him." He smiled, gesturing with
his hand for them to follow him to the maternity ward's
viewing window. When the family was assembled in
front of the glass enclosure, he gestured at the pediat-
ric nurse, who smiled warmly. The woman pushed a
white baby basket to the front and center of the nurs-
ery. She mouthed congratulations at the family as they
all pushed forward to get a glimpse of the new baby.

"We've named him Matthew Jacoby Stallion Jr.," the
new father said proudly. "We're going to call him Jack."

John reached his arms out to hug his brother. "Nice
job," he whispered into the man's ear. "Nice job!"

As the family stood admiring the new bundle of
joy, the beautiful baby resting with a thumb pulled into
his mouth, his eyes squinted as he struggled to focus,
Phaedra tugged on Mason's arm, gesturing for him to
follow her into the hallway.

As the two stepped outside, she tossed a quick
glance back over her shoulder, smiling brightly at the
love and joy that blessed the space.

"What's wrong?" Mason asked, concern falling over his expression.

She shook her head. "Nothing," she said as she reached to wrap her arms around him. "Everything's perfect."

She kissed him keenly, her mouth skating with pleasure over his. "I just wanted to tell you something," she said, the excitement ringing in her tone.

Mason eyed her curiously. "What, baby?"

"I want that," she said, gesturing back to where the family was gathered.

Mason smiled, joy shimmering in his stare as she continued.

"I want family, and you. I want us to have babies together. Lots of babies. I want this life with sisters and brothers and us being a family. I want us to be like your mom and dad, and my brothers and their wives.

"I love you, Mason, and I want to be your wife more than anything else!" she said as she kissed him again.

Holding Phaedra tightly, Mason closed his eyes, pressing a damp kiss against her forehead. He held her as they reveled in the beauty of their love for each other and the love their families had for them both.

Across the room John stood watching them, sensing his sister's happiness, a bright smile blessing his face. Mark met his gaze and nodded his approval as Matthew gave them two thumbs-up. As Phaedra's brothers turned their attention back to the family's celebration, they knew that they would be Stallions forever, forever a family bonded by much more than blood.

* * * * *

REQUEST YOUR FREE BOOKS!

2 FREE NOVELS
PLUS 2 FREE GIFTS!

KIMANI
ROMANCE

Love's ultimate destination!

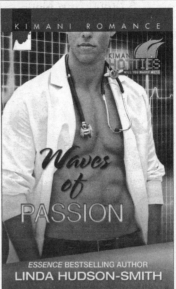

...aris Family Novel!

...STSELLING AUTHOR

BRENDA JACKSON

COURTING JUSTICE

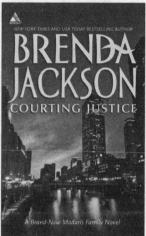

Winning a high-profile case may have helped New York attorney DeAngelo DiMeglio's career, but it hasn't helped him win the woman he loves. Peyton Mahoney doesn't want anything more than a fling with DeAngelo. Until another high-profile case brings them to opposing sides of the courtroom…and then their sizzling attraction can no longer be denied.

"Brenda Jackson is the queen of newly discovered love, especially in her Madaris Family series."
—*BookPage* on *Inseparable*

Available now wherever books are sold.

HARLEQUIN®
www.Harlequin.com

KPBJ4730612F